FIND ME IN PLEASURE

A DARK PLEASURES NOVELLA

MAL & CHRISTINA (PART 2)

BY JULIE KENNER

CHAPTER 1

MY MOTHER KILLED herself when I was seventeen years old.

Not softly with an overdose of pills and then a slide into sweet oblivion. No, she did it brutally. Wildly.

She took a knife. She drew it across her own neck. She sliced her jugular.

She died almost immediately.

I found her about an hour later in the bathtub—her note said she didn't want to stain the grout on the white tiled floor. And it was that one, small nod to propriety that made me cry the hardest.

It takes a lot to slice your own throat. Determination. Strength. And a will of iron.

My mother had all of those things, and I know that I have them, too.

She was also certifiably insane, and my entire life I have feared that I inherited that from her as well.

I fear it now, actually, as I huddle on the ground in a small passage beside my best friend's tony building on Manhattan's Upper East Side. I am wrapped tight in the arms of my lover, my mate. *Malcolm.* A man who I have known for only a few days. Or, perhaps, for over three thousand years.

I am still reeling from a kidnap attempt by a rotund man who had flames where his face should have been.

That man is no longer here in the alley with us. Instead, he is nothing more than a pile of dust on the ground, rendered that way by another man. *Asher.* A man who is supposed to be a friend, and yet who turned on me the moment flame-face was dead, then tried to kill me with a sword made of light. Why? Because there is a weapon inside me. Something dark. Something horrible.

Something that could destroy the world.

But Asher didn't manage to kill me or to destroy the weapon. Instead, he was struck down by Mal, who rescued me with just seconds to spare, driving his own sword of light through Asher just in the nick of time.

But Asher is not dead, either.

Or, rather, he *is* dead. But his body now writhes in a ring of fire. Phoenix fire, to be specific, and it is restoring him to life even as I tremble in Mal's embrace, soaking up his strength and telling myself over and over that I will not cry, I will not cry, I will not cry.

It all sounds pretty damn crazy, doesn't it? Like maybe I truly am my mother's daughter.

Like maybe I am insane and this is all one big psychotic break.

Except it's not.

For all of my twenty-three years, I have been Jaynie Hart, the girl with the crazy mother. The girl who wants to be an actress. Who is only truly happy when she is playing a part.

The girl who fantasizes about seeing her stage name in lights—*Christina Hart*.

But it turns out, that's not a random stage name. It's who I am. Who I have always been.

I'm Christina, and I have been for thousands of years.

I'm Christina, and I'm immortal.

And hundreds of times over the last few millennia, the man that I loved—the man who now holds me close in his arms—killed me again and again and again. Sacrificing me in order to save the world from the vile power that is buried inside me.

But no more.

He's told me he can't do it again. Can't kill me anymore. Not when I finally know who I am. Not when I've finally, after so many lifetimes, remembered him.

And so now it is up to me to keep the weapon deep and safe and buried.

It's up to me to protect the world from a violent power that is fighting to escape.

Honestly, I don't know that I can.

Even with Mal at my side—even with his strength and his love to bolster me—I don't know that I'm that strong.

And, yes, I am scared.

CHAPTER 2

"CHRISTINA. *CHRISTINA*." FROM what seems a very long way away, I hear Mal's voice. Harsh. Urgent.

I blink as he turns me in his arms. And as I look at him, I feel my body go soft in his embrace, the tension and fear that had been building within me tamping down. I breathe deep and focus on his stormy gray eyes, so full of worry. I want to console him—hell, I just want to touch him—and so I reach out and cup my hand against his cheek and the line of his jaw.

The stubble of his beard is rough against my skin as I stroke his face then slide my fingers through his silky mane of coal-black

7

hair, enjoying the raw sensuality of the moment. The beauty of this warrior with the face of a god.

"Christina." His voice is tight and full of concern as he takes my hand and presses a soft kiss to my knuckles. "I need you to say something."

I nod, wanting to both console and reassure. "I'm fine. Really. I'm just overwhelmed."

"And afraid," he says, and somehow the fact that he understands me so well takes the edge off of that fear.

"Yes," I whisper. "But when you hold me it's better."

"I'll never let go," he promises. "But lover, we need to get out of here. There may be more of them coming."

He doesn't have to explain to me who "them" are. He's talking about the fuerie. More creatures like the flame-faced man that Asher killed.

Of course, the fuerie don't really have faces of flame. To regular humans, they appear perfectly normal and can pass through the world unnoticed. It is only those like me and Mal and the rest of the immortals who can see the fuerie as they manifest in this world. A malevolent energy that takes residence within the body of a mortal. A dark force determined to capture me and extract the weapon from me. And, then, of course, to use it.

I draw in a breath and nod, because Mal is right. It's time to get out of here.

It's funny how fast everything in your life can change.

Less than two hours ago, I'd known nothing about the fuerie, nothing about immortality. Instead, I'd been a regular girl, more or less.

I'd been having wild sex in the kitchen, omelette forgotten as I wrapped my legs around Malcolm Greer, the man I'd craved desperately from the first moment I'd seen him. A man who fascinated me. Excited me. Scared me.

A man who two hours ago I hardly

knew, but couldn't resist.

Now I know him well. Now, I remember. Not everything, but enough to know that I trust him.

That he is mine. That I am his.

And that I have been for a very, very long time.

He stands, and as he helps me to my feet, I glance over at the circle of fire inside which Asher is being lashed about as if by a wild wind. Flames lick his body, mixing with his copper-colored hair, and it is obvious that he is almost fully regenerated.

"Is he—? I mean, how much longer before he's whole again?"

I see the battle play out on Mal's face. He wants to get me out of there—and yet despite what Asher did to me—despite the fact that he fully intended to kill me since Mal would not—Asher is still one of the Phoenix Brotherhood. And Mal will not leave a brother behind.

"We wait," I say, answering my own question.

Mal meets my eyes, and I see the appreciation there. The acknowledgment that I understand him. It feels nice, this connection between us, and I sigh a little with satisfaction.

One of Mal's hands is twined in mine. The other is on the hilt of his fire sword, keeping it at the ready. We are both hyperaware of our surroundings. The buildings rising up on either side of us. The trash and recycle bins lining this small passageway. The street noise filtering in from the end of the alley.

It is Sunday morning, and we are alone in this dank, shadowy place. But at the end of the alley, the world is coming to life, and we need to go. Because if the fuerie don't find us soon, surely a mortal will.

As if in echo of my thoughts, I hear the squeal of tires as a car screeches to a halt where the alley meets the street. Even from this distance, I can see that the car is large and black—and that someone is getting out.

Beside me, Malcolm tenses, and I tighten

my grip on his hand. Almost immediately, though, he relaxes, and I am just about to ask him what's going on when I hear a familiar voice. "Now! Come on! There are two more coming—and they're fucking near!"

I see him clearly now, an exceptional man with dark blond hair swept back from his face, golden eyes, and the world's broadest shoulders.

"It's okay," Mal says, turning to me. "This is—"

"Dante," I say, releasing Mal to embrace my old friend. "I remember him."

"Christina?" Dante's smile is like summer. "It's true then? You really do remember everything?"

I shake my head. "Not everything. But a lot." I look at Mal and cannot help but smile. "I remember the most important things at least."

"Right now, the only important thing is getting you out of here."

"You sense more on the way?"

"Sense?" I ask.

"Dante can feel the fuerie," Mal explains.

"Only when they're near," Dante clarifies. "And they are." He points to the car. "Come on. Dennis is at the wheel. We need to move." He frowns toward the circle of fire. Within it, Asher is crouched down, his golden skin dusted with black soot, his back arched and his head bowed. Around him, the flames burn out, leaving only a charred mark on the ground.

"If there are only two, should we take them out?" I ask. "There are four of us now."

"Take her," Mal says to Dante, not even bothering to consider my words. I want to argue, but I don't. Because I know as well as Mal does that fighting isn't really an option. Not for me. Not yet. Not when passion and fear and other wild emotions draw the weapon from where it is buried inside of me. So, yes, I might manage to kill or injure one of the fuerie in a battle. But I might also destroy the entire world in the process.

"Come on." Dante grips my upper arm and starts to pull me away. But I have my eyes locked on Mal and am staying still.

He's taken a step toward Asher who is slowly rising, covered only by the thin layer of soot.

Without warning, Mal lashes out, his fist connecting squarely with Asher's jaw, knocking him back on his ass. I gasp, but neither man looks at me. Beside me, Dante's grip on my arm tightens, and I realize that I've taken a step toward them.

I watch, frozen fast by Dante's iron grip, as Mal stands like an executioner before Asher. "That was for trying to kill my mate." He bends down and grabs Asher's arm and hauls the obviously still weak man to his feet. "This is because I won't leave a brother behind. But Ash, this isn't over."

For a moment, the air all around us seems to shimmer with tension and anticipation. Then Ash meets Mal's eyes, nods, and lets Mal hook his arm around his waist for support.

Despite this tentative détente, the air remains strained. But even that bursts completely when Dante growls, "Enough with the making nice. Can we get the fuck out of here?"

"Go," Mal says, his eyes on me as he starts toward the limo with Asher. "I'm right behind you."

I go, giving in to Dante's demand that I *move now, goddammit*. But it's already too late. All that has happened—Mal holding me, Ash rising, Dante's arrival—has taken less than five minutes. And yet they are already here.

The fuerie.

As Dante warned, there are only two, but they are rushing at us, one on each side of the alley, so that in order to get to the limo, we have to get past them.

Beside me, Dante already has his fire sword extended. And soon the two fuerie become five and the five become ten, as eight more fuerie rush in behind the originals, just as Dante predicted.

Asher's fire sword had fallen to the ground when he died, and now Mal retrieves it. He presses the weapon into Ash's hand, and the two men lock eyes. "Keep her safe," Mal says.

A single beat passes between them, and then Ash nods. A second later, he is at my side. He puts his arm around my shoulders, and I realize that it is not in protection of me, but because he is still weak.

"I'll keep them off us," Ash says, his voice low and raspy. I believe him. But I also realize that without my help, he will most likely not make it to the limo.

I curse, but I don't argue, and I start forward, the two of us stumbling together as Mal and Dante cover us on either side.

The fuerie fight with knives and with a weapon that looks like a whip, but that I soon realize is made of some sort of wire. Even as Dante lashes out with his sword, one of the fuerie flicks his wrist and the wire flies out. But Dante's sword slashes down, and as the fuerie falls, the wire shifts trajectory—and I scream in pain as it slices easily through both my shirt and my flesh.

I fall to the ground, dragging Ash down beside me. My entire body is in agony, so much so that I barely notice the way that Mal has whipped around, his sword outthrust as he spins in a glorious acrobatic move, slicing the heads off of three of the fuerie as he does so.

From what seems like a long distance away, I hear Mal's voice as he shouts to Dante. "Get them! Hurry! I have to get to her before—"

But then I hear nothing more except the rushing in my head.

I feel nothing but the wild power building inside me.

Red hot and bubbling. As if the pain of the wound across my belly and breast is alive and growing and—*oh Christ, oh God*—it's going to explode out of me and I'm screaming for Mal and I'm trying, trying, trying so hard to hold it in. But I can feel the power building and building and the terror inside me growing and growing. And though I try to keep it down, I'm so scared and it's so strong and—

With a *whoosh* everything seems to spill out of me. I go limp, and it is as if there is nothing left inside. Nothing solid that the evil can press against. No purchase it can find inside me in order to climb out.

I breathe deep, relieved and scared and exhausted and hurting all at the same time.

Mal.

I don't understand how, but I know that Mal has calmed the weapon. Pushed it down. And as reality takes form around me again, I realize that I am once again in his arms. Asher stands naked beside him, like a magnificent dusty statue, one hand on Mal's shoulder for support as he holds an extended fire sword in protection over us both.

And Dante—oh, dear god—he is a wild thing, and as I watch he slices through the torsos of the final two fuerie. Their shrieks echo between the buildings, then rise to mix with the sound of traffic and the din of a city coming to life.

Dante's shirt is sliced across the back. Two long, thin strips now soaked with blood. Like me, he'd felt the sting of the fuerie's wire whip, and seeing his wound now makes the deep slice down my own body throb with renewed pain.

"We'll get you both to Jessica," Mal says. "She'll tend to these wounds."

He looks up to meet Asher's eyes. "Can you get to the limo on your own?"

Ash nods. "Just take care of Christina. I can help Dante finish them off. We're right behind you."

Mal nods, then scoops me up and cradles me against his chest. As he walks toward the limo that blocks and fills the entrance to the alleyway, I look back and see Dante and Asher stabbing each of the fallen fuerie through the heart—and as soon as they do, the fuerie turn to dust, leaving no evidence of the battle other than piles of ash and some blood staining the asphalt.

I tremble in Mal's arms.

"Christina?"

I hear the fear in his voice. "I'm okay," I assure him as he puts me on my feet and helps me into the limo.

He gets in beside me then presses a kiss to my forehead. "Rest now. Whatever questions you have can wait."

I nod, thinking about how little I know of this man despite the fact that I know him so well. Even now that my memories are coming back, I still do not have the full picture of him. Because for thousands of years I have not been with him. And a lot can happen in three millennia, even for creatures such as us, for whom time does not mean the same thing as it does to humans.

I realize only when the limo starts to pull away that not only has someone closed the door, but that Dante and Asher aren't with us. "Where—?"

"They're up front," Mal says. "Just rest."

I do, leaning against him, breathing him in, and letting memories crash over me like waves. The way that we had left our home in another dimension to cross time and space as we chased the fuerie, on a mission to not only capture it, but to reclaim the weapon that it had stolen.

The accident that had thrust both us and our quarry off-course, sending us hurtling across the void and into this dimension.

The desperate need for form, because this world cannot support beings like us composed of pure, sentient energy.

We'd merged then with willing humans—bonded with them and become flesh.

I remember discovering the incredible sensations of touch. The indescribable beauty of taste. The experience of interpreting sound waves through a body. And oh, dear god, the wonder of looking upon the sensual, beautiful form of Mal's human self.

Mal and I had only one glorious, delicious night together to explore our new forms. To touch and taste and tease.

Even now, I can remember the way it felt in his arms-real and warm and vibrant. So much richer than when we had mated in our dimension, twining our essences as we shared ourselves.

And I can remember the taste of fear and of pain when the fuerie had captured me. When they'd violated me. When they'd thrust their weapon deep inside me, because in this universe energy cannot go unbound, and the fuerie had needed a vessel to contain such an enormous and feral power.

I remember the battle that followed, and I remember being rescued.

And I remember the pain and the horror of that first night, when Mal realized what was inside me. What was building. What was about to burst out of me.

And, of course, I remember when he killed me.

Now, in his arms, I tremble.

"Hush," he says, stroking my hair. "I've asked Dennis to just drive for a bit. I don't want to go straight back in case we're being tailed. The fuerie are aware of Number 36 already," he adds, referring to the building owned by the brotherhood on East 63rd Street. "But they don't understand its importance."

I nod. Number 36 is also the location for Dark Pleasures, a members-only scotch and cigar club that had been established in 1895. But the club is only one facet of the property, and though I do not know the details of what the brotherhood has built over the last three thousand years, I realize that excellent drinks, fine cigars, and good company is the least of what goes on within those walls.

With a nod, I close my eyes again, willing the exhaustion to draw me back down. But I cannot let go. I can't shake the memory of what I saw in that alley. The battle. The risk.

What if Mal had been cut down by the fuerie's whip? What if he weren't immortal?

What if I lost him?

I feel the hot press of tears burn in my eyes. "You've had to kill me so many times," I whisper, then feel his body go tense against mine, as if he is waiting for a blow. I turn in his arms and look at his face. At the self-loathing in his eyes.

"No," I whisper as a tear snakes down my cheek. I lift my hand to brush my fingertips across his lip. "No, I'm not—" I draw a breath to gather my thoughts. "Don't you see? I may have died over and over again, but you had the worst of it. Oh, god, Mal, I can't imagine losing you even once, and yet you had to walk through hell over and over and over again. And you had to inflict that hell on yourself. I don't know how you survived it."

"I couldn't." His voice is gravelly with emotion. "I didn't." He pulls me close and kisses me hard. "I couldn't do it again. I couldn't destroy you this time."

I swallow, my eyes locked on his, my breathing hard. And then slowly I turn and look at the front of the limo, where I know that Asher sits behind the privacy panel. "I know what's inside me, Mal. And I don't know if I can control it. No," I amend, remembering the horror I'd felt only moments ago as the heat and power had risen inside me for the third—*third*—time that morning. "No, I know that I *can't* control it."

He takes my hands, holding them tight in his as he looks at me. "I told you to trust me to help you," he says. "You said that you did."

"I did. I do." I draw in a breath. "But you need to tell me what we're going to do."

His smile is slow and sexy and just a little bit devious. "Lover, I'm going to do better than that. I'm going to show you."

CHAPTER 3

"SHE'LL BE FINE," Mal said to Jessica, as if by making the statement, he could make it so. He glanced quickly at Dante, who sat on the couch in Mal's second floor den, bent forward with his elbows on his knees so that his marred back was exposed. "Both of them will be fine."

In front of him, Jessica tucked a loose strand of wavy black hair behind her ear and bent closer to Christina, whom he still held tight in his arms. "Just a quick look," Jessica said gently to Christina. "I promise this won't hurt."

It already hurt—that much Mal knew damn well. How could a fuerie's whip not hurt? But to her credit, Christina nodded, her bone-deep exhaustion painted across her face. Then she bit her lower lip as Jessica gently moved the ripped shirt out of the way so that she could better examine the injury.

The wound was long and thin, like a slice from a razor, and the sight of it marring Christina's soft skin made Mal's gut clench.

This was his fault. He should have gotten her out of the alley immediately. He should have left Ash to fend for himself.

He should have protected Christina.

Gently, he held her close, bending his head over hers and brushing his lips over her forehead. Only when he felt the soft press of Jessica's palm against his shoulder did he look up.

"She's going to be fine," Jessica said. "Just like you said. Now go put her on the bed while I deal with Dante."

"No," he said. "In here." He was damned if he was taking her into his bed wounded. His bed was the place to help her. To heal her. Hell, to cherish her. He wasn't about to mar the sanctity of that place by tainting it with this goddamn major fuck-up.

Dammit, dammit, dammit.

He'd caused that wound as efficiently as if he'd wielded the whip himself.

He'd hurt her.

And that reality ripped him to shreds.

He moved to sit in a chair, not because it strained him to hold her slim body, but because the weight of his guilt was almost too heavy to bear.

"Mal." Christina's whisper was thin and weak.

"What?" He bent his head, trying to hear her better.

"Stop worrying about me." Her lips curved, and that sweet smile warmed him to his core.

"Never," he said, but he realized that she'd made him feel better. Ironic, he thought, since she was the one who was wounded.

A few feet away, Dante rose from the couch, the two cuts on his back now clean and bandaged. He turned to look at Mal. "Debrief in thirty?"

Mal glanced down at Christina, then shook his head. "We'll meet at four." According to the huge grandfather clock he'd acquired in London over three centuries ago, it wasn't yet noon. That would give him a full four hours alone with Christina. And dear god, he needed it. "Tell Liam and the rest for me, will you? We'll convene in the courtyard."

"You got it." He balled up his shredded shirt, then tossed it in the wastebasket. "Thanks, Jessica."

"My pleasure. Tell Liam I'll be right back." Her grin was pure wickedness. "Four entire hours free. What *will* we do with ourselves?"

As Dante rolled his eyes and took the stairs down to the entry level of Mal's six story brownstone, Jessica turned her attention to Christina.

"You don't have to hold her," Jessica said gently. "This isn't going to hurt."

"Is holding her a problem?" He knew that *not* holding her would be a problem, at least for him. Right at the moment, the thought of releasing her seemed like the hardest thing anyone could ask him to do.

The corner of Jessica's mouth twitched. "No," she said gently. "Hold onto her for as long as you need."

A good answer, Mal thought. Because that was exactly what he intended to do.

I'M SO TIRED that I say nothing when Mal says that he will hold me while Jessica cleans my wound and bandages me up.

I don't understand why I am so exhausted, but I feel as if I could sleep for a year. As if all of my energy has been drained right out of me. I'm so tired, in fact, that when we arrived, I barely noticed the inside of Mal's house, a lovely brownstone that is connected to Number 36 by a charming courtyard.

I'd seen the courtyard before, and I'd

assumed the brownstone had been converted to multiple apartments.

I'd been wrong.

Instead, it's an absolutely stunning building, full of polished wood and fabulous
artwork and a mix of both contemporary
and antique furniture that should clash, but
really doesn't. Instead, it's like Mal himself,
the building and the interior reflecting both
the facets of the man and the years through
which his has lived.

At some point, I want him to take me
through every room on every floor. I want
to see his souvenirs and hear about his
memories. Right now, though, as he holds
me in his arms in this comfortable den with
plush furniture in shades of brown and
ivory, all I want to do is close my eyes and
float away.

"Sleepy," I say as I snuggle closer to the
warmth of his chest.

"I know you are, lover. I'll give some of
it back as soon as Jessica's finished."

I frown up at him, not understanding his

words. But I see no explanation in those steel gray eyes, and before I can ask what he means, Jessica is very gently cutting off my T-shirt with a pair of small scissors.

"It's really not that bad a wound," I say, though in truth the pain that had faded when Mal pushed the weapon back down is starting to return.

"Maybe not. But unless you let me treat it, you'll not only have pain but a nasty scar."

I frown and glance over toward the stairs down which Dante had descended only moments before, his wound treated with nothing more than ointment and Bandaids. Jessica, to her credit, laughs.

"Oh, please. A scar only makes him look like more of a badass. And the truth is, if he bites it in a fight, the phoenix fire is going to fix any lingering scar, anyway. But you don't need to look like a bad ass."

"She certainly doesn't," Mal says.

What neither of them say is that the phoenix fire would do nothing for me. If I die, then I'm gone. For a year, a hundred, a thousand. Who knows? And who knows when I would find Mal again?

His arms tighten around me, and I know that he is thinking the same thing.

"So what are you going to do?" I ask Jessica.

Her smile is devilishly wide. "I'm going to fix you." She glances toward Mal. "It's Sunday morning, and I'm missing brunch. Surely you could spare a mimosa? And I think Christina could use one, too."

"Jessica…"

I think I hear a warning in his voice, but she only ignores it, which makes me like her all the more. Mal, after all, is not an easy man to defy.

"Oh, go on," she says. "I promise not to do a thing until she's back in your arms."

Mal sighs, but I see the flicker of amusement cross his face before he gently settles me in the huge armchair. As soon as he's in the kitchen, I turn my attention to Jessica. "No offense, but if you think you're going to stitch me up while drinking, you are seriously misinformed."

"No stitches," Jessica says. "Promise."

I frown. I may not know much about wounds and scars, but I do know that unless this one is taken care of, that badass scar she said I didn't need would be right there across my torso, a nasty, puckered reminder of today's unpleasant encounter with the bad guys.

"Tell her, Mal," Jessica demands as Mal returns with two champagne glasses filled with mimosas and one highball glass filled with scotch. "Tell her that I'll get her back to perfect."

"She's already perfect," he counters, then turns to me. "But I will tell you that she'll fix that wound up nicely."

Jessica rolls her eyes. "Good enough." She takes the glass Mal offers, and I watch as she downs it in one long swallow. He hands me mine next, then sits on the arm of the chair and takes my hand with his free one, twining our fingers together. "Lie back, lover. Let her take care of you."

I hesitate, then take a long sip of my drink before complying so that I am sprawled on the chair, my head back and my feet up on the ottoman. Since I can hardly drink while I'm like this, Jessica takes my glass and downs the orange juice and champagne cocktail before setting the glass aside.

"Trust me," she says. "A little alcohol only helps me out. Loosens me up. Lets the energy flow more freely."

I meet Mal's eyes, certain that Jessica must be teasing me. But all he does is nod. "Energy is the root of everything in the universe." His voice is steady. Soothing. And I realize that he's speaking not only to instruct, but also to make sure I stay calm. "Do you remember that much?"

"I think so," I say, though I'm not sure if I'm remembering middle school science or deeper lessons from a life I recall only in pieces.

"Good. And even in this world, where sentient beings require matter in order to function, energy remains at the heart of it. And we, Christina, started out as beings of pure energy."

As he speaks, Jessica's fingers are skimming over me, her focus intent as she examines the wound.

The truth is that I only understand part of what he is saying. The things that I have remembered are moments, not theory or philosophy or the underlying answer to questions about the very nature of existence. Instead, I remember the battle when we crashed. The times that Mal destroyed me. The pain when the fuerie put the weapon inside me. I remember things that happened to me or because of me. But I have very little understanding of what—or who—that "me" really is.

"Everything you can see, feel, taste, touch," Mal continues, not noticing that my attention has wandered. "There's energy at the core of it. Does that make sense?"

I nod.

"Every cell, every atom," Jessica adds.

"Hell, even every memory."

"Jess." Mal's voice is surprisingly terse.

She cuts a glance toward him, then smiles in what I think is apology. "Anyway, it all goes back to energy. Look," she says. "All I'm doing is manipulating energy."

I glance down to where Jessica's fingertip is tracing very slowly along the line of my wound, which is turning slightly pink as the skin knits together behind her touch.

"How are you—"

Her smile is gentle. "Everyone in the brotherhood manifests a control over energy, though we each have different strengths. My particular skill is healing."

"And here I assumed you'd just gone to med school."

"Well, that too." She grins. "You're all done."

I look again, amazed that my skin appears entirely unmarred. "Wow."

"I'm glad you're pleased," Jessica says.

I manage a nonchalant lift of a shoulder. "Well, I was hoping to look like a badass, but if this is the best that you can do…"

She laughs, then glances between me and Mal. "She's still wiped out, and I just drained her even more."

"I'll take care of her," he says.

"I know you will. And I'll see the two of you at four. In the meantime," she adds with another wicked little smile, "enjoy your Sunday. I know Liam and I intend to enjoy ours."

And then she's gone, her light footsteps echoing as she descends the stairs. A moment later, I hear a door open, and then very firmly shut again.

"Has there ever been a sweeter sound?" Mal rises from the arm of the chair to stand beside me. "I finally have you all to myself."

He pulls the ottoman back, then gently puts my feet on the floor. I start to scoot up a bit, intending to adjust my position so that I am sitting more than sprawling.

"No."

Just that one word, but it locks me into place. I lick my lips, suddenly breathing hard. Suddenly aware of all sorts of decadent possibilities. "Mal…"

He says nothing, but he meets my eyes as he drops to his knees between the ottoman and the chair. All around me, the air feels warm and heavy. *Energy.* Was this what Jessica meant? Because right at the moment, the heat that Mal is generating could fuel a small nation.

Slowly, he puts his hands on my knees, and even through my jeans, his touch is electric, sending sparks running through my entire body, making me moan. I shift my hips a bit, feeling antsy and needy, and as I do I realize that I am wet.

My legs are parted, and though I'm still wearing my jeans, I feel exposed. I'm in only my bra, and where that had seemed fine just moments before, now I am on edge. My nipples are hard. My body on fire. I am not used to this sensation—to wanting a man so badly that my body opens to him with so little provocation. The feeling that I should be naked.

The knowledge that I am his to do with as he wants.

And the sweet, terrifying, undeniable truth that I crave everything that he might do to me.

CHAPTER 4

I CROSS MY arms over my chest, suddenly overwhelmed by the depth of my own desire. "I—I need a shirt."

The corner of Mal's mouth twitches. "You really don't," he says, looking at me with such sensual intensity that I'm pretty sure any shirt I might put on would immediately be burned off.

"Mal—"

"Tell me what you really need." As he speaks, his hands are sliding up my thighs, slowly, slowly, so painfully slowly.

I swallow, not sure I am capable of forming words.

"Do you want me to stop touching

you?"

"*No.*" The word is ripped from me.

"Then what?" His thumbs stroke the juncture of my thighs, one on each side of my sex, and even through the denim the sensation is pure, decadent delight.

"It's just that I've never felt this way before." The admission surprises me. Not because it's true, but because I am admitting that to Mal.

"Tell me," he says. "How do you feel?"

"Open," I admit.

"And?"

I meet his eyes, nerves fluttering in my chest. But I push forward, because it's important to say the words. "I trust you," I say. My words are barely a whisper, but I see the fire they spark in him, and I do not regret speaking.

"I'm glad."

I manage a small smile. "It's a little terrifying," I say, and he laughs, the sound acting like a balm and easing the last of the tension out of me. That heavy exhaustion still lingers, but I blame that on the injury and Jessica's treatment. And even if I were bone tired, I wouldn't care. Because I want more. I want everything.

Hell, I just want Mal.

His hands slide up and I tremble as his fingers find the button of my jeans. He unfastens it, then slowly tugs the zipper down and starts to slide them off, using one hand to lift my hips.

"And just what exactly are you doing?" My voice is low and husky, and the little half-smile on my lips is playful.

He chuckles. "Lover, I think you know."

He has a point.

He tosses my sandals and jeans aside, leaving me clad only in tiny thong panties and my lacy bra. He glances at the pile of clothing and then back at me. "Then again, perhaps I'm doing more than you think."

What I think is that he's going to send me ricocheting off the moon. And what he's doing seems to be proving that out. His hands are on my thighs, stroking my skin slowly—so painfully slowly. And in the wake of each caress, I feel a tingle, almost like a pinched nerve coming back to life.

"Mal? Oh, god, Mal, that feels wonderful." Whatever it is, the heaviness that had settled over me and had been pulling me inexorably toward sleep has faded, replaced now with a wonderful energy. Sexual, yes, but more than that. I feel amazing.

Hell, I feel alive.

I moan with pleasure. "Whatever you're doing, don't stop."

"I'm giving back what I took," he says. "Just like the doctor ordered."

I'm about to ask what he means when he bends his head to my leg, and suddenly his mouth is where his hand was only moments before. He's kissing the soft skin of my inner thigh, moving higher and higher, his tongue and lips teasing me, sending sparks dancing through me, making my body tense and my pulse skitter.

I cling to the armrest, then to his hair. And then—oh, dear god—his mouth closes over the crotch of my panties and he uses his finger to tug the tiny scrap of material aside so that his tongue can stroke my sex, laving me, tasting me, then teasing my clit ever so gently. And I feel the world start to spiral up, up, up.

And as it does, I remember what happened the last time he got me this excited.

I stiffen, putting my hands on his head and pushing him away. "Mal. No. No, you can't."

I'm breathing hard again, but now it's not sexual excitement, it's fear. I want his touch—dear god, how I want it—but I know I can't have it. "My apartment," I say, the words coming on a gasp. "Before I ran to the alley. Before I knew the truth."

I remember the power surging inside me. The wildness.

"That wasn't just the world's most amazing orgasm, was it? That was the weapon." I shudder. "It was building in me."

I see the truth in his eyes, but I don't even need that to know that I'm right. I'd felt the same intensity in the alley when Asher threatened me. A sense that I was going to explode and take the world with me.

A feeling that didn't dissipate until Mal struck Asher down and gathered me in his arms.

I push myself up so that I am sitting and curl my legs under me. If there had been a blanket, I would have hidden beneath it.

In front of me, Mal moves slowly onto the ottoman. He says nothing, only waits for me to compose myself. And despite everything, I appreciate that small courtesy.

It takes a moment or two, but I finally gather my control. "That's your power, isn't it? You can control the weapon."

"No," he says, dashing the tentative relief that had been blooming within me. "But I can control you."

I frown, confused, and hug myself. "What do you mean?"

"I could mean a lot of things." He moves from the ottoman to sit on the edge of the chair with me, then lightly trails his finger over my shoulder. "I could mean that I can make you wet." He eases his finger lower, tracing the curve of my breast along my bra cup. "It could mean that I can make you beg."

"Mal..." My voice doesn't sound like my own. It sounds needy. Desperate. And I am not at all certain if I want him to stop or to continue.

What I want doesn't matter, though, as he is still following his path, down, down, down, over my stomach and then to the band of my thong. My legs are curled under me, but all he does is close his hands over each of my thighs and very slowly ease them apart.

I actually whimper, and then—as that dangerous finger slides lower to stroke my clit through the thin, soaked satin—I bite my lip. "Mal." His name is soft, and this time there is a desperation in my tone. Not sensual, but fearful. Because I can feel the wildness building inside me again. "*Mal.*"

"Trust me," he says, as he slips his fingers beneath the satin and thrusts into me. I arch up, almost crying both from pleasure and from the line that we are skirting, and I'm trying—trying so damn hard not to get excited. Not to let the pleasure build in me. Not to feel the power rise, the heat, the onslaught of the kind of explosion that we truly won't survive, but—

And then it's gone.

The rising pressure has receded, and I'm left gasping, my body still flush and aware, but softer now, tired. As if I came without noticing it and now I'm warm and sated.

"What happened?"

"I drew off some of your energy." His voice is soft and steady. Soothing. And as he speaks, he holds my hand. "The weapon is inside you—that means it's primed by your energy. Your emotions, your power. You stay in control, then so does the weapon. Lose control—through sex, through anger, through fear—and your energy pushes the weapon up. Too much, and it will generate its own power."

"It's own power?"

He shrugs. "A theory, but a good one. Within you, the weapon is dormant. It needs energy, so it draws from you when it can, filling its own reserve. But there's a tipping point when it has drawn enough from you and can exist on its own, no longer a parasite."

"Oh." I'm not really liking that analogy, but I understand what he's saying. Sort of, anyway.

"When the weapon was going hot, I didn't take the weapon's energy, I took yours. And that backed it off. And now," he adds, stroking me again, "I'm giving that energy back to you." He meets my eyes. "Do you understand?"

I nod. Not only do I understand it, I feel it. The lazy, languid sensation is gone, replaced by a vibrancy that has me feeling anything but exhausted. "Mal, please," I beg as he slows his hands.

"Hush," he says, tracing small circles on

my thighs. "I'm not finished telling you how I'm going to help you keep the weapon at bay."

He slides to the ground in front of me then moves his hands to my breasts. He doesn't unfasten my bra, but he does slide the cup down, then closes his mouth over my breast and strokes his tongue over my nipple.

I actually mewl. And when his hand slides between my legs to cup my sex even as his teeth graze my nipple, I arch up, my body shifting as if to escape this onslaught of pleasure, but I'm trapped by his hand and his mouth, this chair like a prison of delights. And as the sensation grows I gasp, wanting the release of an orgasm even as the dark power that is rising inside fills me with terror.

And then, as quickly as his mouth closed over me, he backs off. Not taking my energy this time, but just leaving me breathing hard and feeling hot and wet and needy.

"Good girl," he says, with a smug little

smile.

"What the hell?" This is not the time for polite inquiries.

But all he says is, "Trust me."

"Mal." I grind his name out like a curse.

He says nothing. But once more, his fingers stroke me, teasing me through my thong, then beneath it, then sliding his fingers inside me until I am gasping with pleasure, my body clutching around him, silently begging him for more. For *him*.

"Christ, you're so responsive. I swear I can't resist you."

"Then fuck me, Mal. Please. I want to feel you inside me."

"Soon," he promises. "Right now, I want to enjoy watching you. The way you move when I touch you. Your soft moans that make me so hard."

"Yes," I murmur.

"Do you have any idea what I want to do to you?"

I draw in a trembling breath and close my eyes. "Tell me."

"I want to take you to the edge. I want to lead you right to the precipice, and then I want to look you in the eye as you fight to keep from coming."

"Fight?"

"That's just it, lover. You don't come until I say you can."

My eyes flutter open. "I'm not sure I like this game."

"Do you trust me?"

"I thought I did, but I'm thinking I should take that back."

He laughs. "You want my help to control the weapon inside you, right? Well, we're going to do that by me taking control of you."

My entire body goes warm, and I swallow. "Control?"

"Control," he says, and the word is as potent as a caress. "This will work, lover." He strokes his fingers over my skin, and I almost melt with longing. "You learn sexual control, and you can translate that into control of the weapon."

I frown, uncertain.

"Trust me," he says. "This will work."

I lift a brow. "Except I never get an orgasm?"

He chuckles. "Oh, you do. We're just going to take it slowly. Carefully. And very, very deliberately." As he speaks, he touches me, and I cannot deny that his plan is tempting. It may even work.

"I guess we might as well try," I finally say. "At the very least, it'll be interesting." As far as I'm concerned, "interesting" is a synonym for "sexually frustrating."

"Lover," he promises, "it will be exquisite. Dancing along that precipice. Holding your submission in my hand. The pressure building, the need growing—and then the sweetness when you finally do get satisfaction, when we are both sure. And when I am right there to bring it down if you get out of control."

I draw in a breath, both turned on and relieved. Because he is right. With Malcolm beside me, I can do this. I can hold back. I can exercise control.

And if I fail, he will be there to save me. To save us all.

"Okay?" He is looking at me intently, as if his whole world waits on my decision. And in a way I guess it does.

"Okay," I say. "But we can't start now." I'm fighting a smile, and it's very obvious that he realizes as much.

"No? Why not?"

"The situation is inequitable."

A muscle in his cheek twitches, but other than that, he doesn't react. "Inequitable?"

"Here I am, practically naked. And there you are, entirely clothed."

"I see." His voice is thoughtful. "Perhaps you missed the whole submission part of the equation. You're mine to command."

"I know that. I just thought perhaps submission came with a view." I bat my eyes and conjure what I hope is a seductive smile. "Unless you're the shy type?"

He says nothing, but he does stand up.

For a moment, I'm afraid that I've shifted the balance of power in this little game and he's going to leave. And considering how turned on I am at the moment, that really wasn't my intent. But he only stands there in that space between ottoman and chair.

And then—oh, heaven help me—he strips.

The shirt comes off first, and I draw in a breath of appreciation. We'd made love in my best friend's kitchen just this morning—was it only this morning?—but he'd kept his T-shirt on. Now, I see the broad chest, firm and tanned. The light dusting of chest hair that starts at his pecs and arrows down to hidden treasure below his still fastened waistband. His skin is smooth and tight, and I want to draw my fingers over it. To feel the tension and the heartbeat.

Mostly, though, I want to trace my fingertip over the exquisite bird that is tattooed in vibrant colors, the tail feathers trailing down to curve into his waist as a hint of flames flicker up from beneath the waistband of his jeans.

"A phoenix," I whisper. "You only have one?"

His brow furrows. "You remember?"

I shake my head, because I don't understand why I asked the question. But even as I'm about to tell him that I don't know where that came from, I realize that I do remember. I hadn't noticed on Asher because he'd been too covered in soot and I hadn't been paying that much attention. I'd seen enough to know that the man was beyond gorgeous, but considering that I'm with Mal and that Asher had tried to kill me, it had seemed rude to stare.

"It's the mark," I say. "The tat grows with every death." I meet his eyes. "How many times have you died, Mal?"

"Not many. Only twenty-seven."

The number slices through me. Any death is too many, as far as I'm concerned, even knowing that he comes back. I rise to stand in front of him and press my fingertip to the bird's majestic head. He takes my hand and guides it down, tracing the magnificent tail feathers. "Eight deaths in the tail," he says, then turns so that I am looking at his back where two birds preside over his shoulders, their beaks meeting at his spine. "The rest in those two and their feathers."

I press my hands to his back, then draw my lips down his spine. I do not know why it hurts so much—perhaps it is a reminder of all that he has suffered while we have been apart—all I know is that I want to fold myself in his arms. That I want to kiss it and make it better. But there is no way to change the past, and all we can do now is move forward.

He turns back around, and I tilt my head up to look at him, and then gasp as he pulls me close, capturing me in a wild kiss full of passion and promise. His mouth is hard against mine, his tongue tasting and taking, and I open to him, my whole body going soft and wet with need.

His hands are on my back, and with one

nimble movement he unfastens my bra. He is not nearly so gentle with my thong—he simply rips the panties right off me. Nor am I gentle, either. My fingers fumble for the button of his jeans, and I have to force myself to skim the zipper down gently so that I do not injure him. And then, once he is naked, I can only stare, astounded by the perfection of this man and by the knowledge that he belongs to me. That of all the women in the world, I alone have the right to touch and taste and enjoy.

And I intend to do exactly that.

I move closer, then press my lips to the delicate line of hair that trails downward, intending to follow that path to heaven. But Mal has other plans, and he pulls me to my feet even as he moves to the chair I've abandoned. He sits, leaning back so that his hard, thick cock lays against his abdomen. "Come here, lover," he says. "Knees on either side of me. And then," he adds as I start eagerly toward him, "I want your legs over the armrests."

"What?"

"You heard me. Straddle the chair. Straddle me."

My entire body goes limp at the prospect, but I comply. It is an insanely sensual position. My legs wide, so that I am beyond vulnerable. His cock right there at my slit, teasing me but not entering me.

Between us, the air is wild and hot, full of all that energy that Jessica was talking about. So thick with passion that I feel as though the damn chair could evaporate and I would stay right here, buoyed by the heat that fills this space between us.

And then he manages to set fire to the world even more by leaning forward and easing the tip of his cock inside me. Just enough to tease. Just enough to torment.

I arch back, wanting to squirm, but his hands close fast around my hips, holding me in this position.

"Don't move," he orders, even as he pulls one of his hands away, then slides it between us to stroke me.

"Mal." I let my head fall back, over-whelmed by the riot of sensation coursing through my body. Delicious sparks that are filling me and spreading through me. "Oh, yes, Mal."

I feel myself tremble as the passion rises. "No," he says. "Don't come." And yet he does not lessen the onslaught, and every-thing inside me is building to a fever pitch. But I *have* to control it. This isn't just a sex game, it's survival. And I know that when we meet with the others in just a few hours, we need to be able to tell them that I'm learning control—not necessarily *how*, but we need to honestly say that I am learning to hold the weapon down.

Even as these thoughts roll through my head, Mal's mouth closes over my breast. At the same time, he takes me by the waist and moves me forward. "Knees on the chair," he demands, and I comply so that I am no longer straddling the armrests, but am kneeling over him. As soon as I'm in this new position, he takes my hips, then pushes me down even as he thrusts up. I cry out, losing myself to the glorious sensation of being impaled upon the hard length of his cock.

"That's it," he says as he teases my clit with his finger even as he finds a rhythm for our joined bodies. "Just a little closer."

"Mal—" His name is both a plea and an admonishment. "What are you doing? We can't—I can't—"

"My job is to try to make you come," he whispers. "To take you higher. To push you to the edge. And your job," he adds as he moves his hand from my clit to my nipple and then twists slightly, sending sparks of pleasure and pain ricocheting through me, "is to hold back."

I want to curse, but I can't spare the focus. I have to concentrate instead on what he's doing. On what I'm *not* doing. Because I have to do this. I have to fight my own desire—my own body—and damn him, he's not helping at all.

Except, of course, he is.

Because that's the point, isn't it? This exercise isn't just about keeping the weapon from rising, it's about keeping me with Mal. It's about what Asher tried to do and the fact that right now, I am under Mal and Liam's protection. Because though I do not remember everything, I do remember that Mal and Liam are a team—that they lead the brotherhood jointly. Which means that if I'm in Mal's protection, I am also in Liam's.

But if we—*if I*—can't prove that I can control this thing inside me, Liam will change his mind. He'll side with Asher. And while I know that Liam and Mal have led the brotherhood since this mission began in another world and another time, I also know that I could be the catalyst that changes all that. That forces Mal out and Asher in.

That condemns me to death yet again.

I want to say all of that, and yet I can't, because Mal is inside me, filling me, and his hands are upon me. His lips are destroying me. He's setting my body on fire and in a minute all of this will be moot because there is no way I can fight this riot of sensations. This storm that is about to burst over me, and is driving me up, building and rising and—

Oh god. Oh no.

"Don't." His voice is intense. Hard. Commanding. And I cling to it. Using his strength to build my own, even as he relentlessly torments my body, his hands and mouth and cock playing and teasing and tormenting me, urging me to come hard and come fast even as that one word rings through me. *Don't.*

And it's building and growing—and not just the pleasure of an orgasm, but the dark fire of the weapon, too, and *oh god, oh Christ.* "I can't. I can't."

"You can," he says, his touch relentless. "Lover, you can."

I breathe deep, trying to focus—to fight—despite the riot inside me.

I try to imagine Mal's touch—his power. I pretend that instead of tempting me, he is helping me. Pulling it back. Pushing it down.

And then—

—and then it all starts to fall away.

Oh god oh god oh god.

It worked.

I still feel edgy and wild. I am still walking a precipice. But now it feels safe. Now I am steady.

I breathe deep, pulling it in, and when I look at Mal, I can't help but laugh in delight at the wide, proud smile I see on his face.

"You did it."

"I am so damn horny," I admit, and his laugh joins mine.

I draw in a breath and then shift off of his still-hard cock.

He chuckles. "That hardly seems fair."

I smirk, feeling playful. "Hey, I don't get to come. You don't get to come."

"Definitely doesn't feel fair," he says, but he moves over in the chair so that I can snuggle up against him.

"Well, maybe I'll change my mind in a bit," I say. "If you're very, very nice to me."

"I'm very proud of you. Does that

work?"

"It's a start," I say, and then kiss him.

We stay that way for a while, warm in each other's arms, and I like it. It feels nice. Comfortable. Gentle, and yet sensual. A little bit erotic, and yet safe.

After a moment, I stretch. "I'm not even tired," I say. "I thought that I'd feel the way I do when you back it down."

"I'm taking energy from you when I back it off," he says. "But I didn't take anything from you just now. All you did was redirect your own power."

I shift a bit to face him. "So when you take the energy, is it yours? I mean, you can use it?"

"I can. It can fuel me. Or I can return it—to you or someone else who is in need of it. And when the need is very great, I can send it back out into the world instead of into a person."

"I have no idea what you mean."

His brows furrow as he considers. "I guess you'd call it a forcefield."

"Yeah? That's cool."

"It requires a massive effort. I don't do it often." He frowns slightly, his gaze hard on me. "Only when the need is important."

"Oh." I think about all that he's told me, but I'm an actress and not a physicist, and I don't completely get how it works. And while I do realize that deep inside of me is a woman with a much more cohesive understanding of all that, I've already reached far enough into myself today. The holes in my memory of our life together trouble me, but right now, I don't intend to dig deeper.

The thought, however, makes me melancholy. Not because I don't recall the intricate workings of energy, but because I have lost so much of my life with Mal. Hell, so much of my life, period. Thousands of years, and what I remember is so fleeting, that each tiny thought and flash is precious to me.

I frown, reminded of something that Jessica said earlier. About energy. About

Pickering Public Library
pickering.bibliocommons.com

Items that you have checked out

Title: Find me in pleasure : Mal & Christin
ID: 33081500204335
Due: May-02-16

Title: Find me in passion : Mal & Christina
ID: 33081500204343
Due: May-02-16

Total items: 2
Account balance: 0
11/04/2016 12:56 PM
Checked out: 5
Overdue: 0
Hold requests: 2
Ready for pick up: 0

Thank you for using the Pickering Public
Library
Automated Phone Renewal 905-831-8209
Central Branch 905-831-6265

memories.

I shift so that I am facing Mal directly. "You can take memories, too, can't you?"

I don't need his verbal confirmation to know that I'm right. The expression on his face gives me all the answer I need.

"Oh, god," I say, sitting up straighter. "You've taken mine."

"Christina—"

But I hold up a hand to cut him off. I frown as I recall the dream I'd awakened from just a few mornings ago. A sensual dream about a gray eyed man. His mouth on mine. His hands on me. I'd awakened aroused, believing it to be only an erotic dream. A fantasy.

But it wasn't. It wasn't a dream, but the wispy remnants of a memory.

"I want it back," I whisper. "Christ, Mal, I want my memories back."

"I'm so sorry," he says. "It doesn't work that way."

CHAPTER 5

I AM OFF his lap in seconds. "I want them back," I repeat.

But he just shakes his head and looks at me with eyes filled with sadness.

I run my fingers through my hair and pace to the couch. There is a small afghan there, and I wrap it around myself, feeling suddenly, strangely exposed.

"Christina, please."

"Please, what?" I ask, turning to him. My temper is ripe, my emotions a jumble. I feel violated. The me that I thought I knew isn't really that girl at all. There are moments missing. Pieces of my life that are gone because someone else chose to take them.

"You can't do that," I say. "You can't just steal bits of my life from me."

I think of my mother and the weeks—even months—that she would simply lose. Forgetting that I'd had a friend over. Forgetting that we'd celebrated Christmas. Forgetting movies and talks. Just … forgetting.

And my own fugues. *Oh, god.* Were those blank moments in my childhood because of Mal?

I turn accusing eyes toward him. "Did you come to me when I was a child? Did you steal my memories even then? How many times did you kill me when I was still a child?"

"*Never.*" The word is hard. Vehement. "I have only sensed you as an adult. I don't know why. Perhaps the weapon stays dormant until then. I didn't—hell, I couldn't—"

"Couldn't?" I can't keep the harsh edge out of my voice. "Sounds to me like you're capable of quite a lot."

I look at him, still in the chair, but his hands are so tight on the armrests that his knuckles appear white. His face is tense, his expression stony. He is holding his temper in, but just barely.

And I am not in the mood to coddle.

There may well be an explosion tonight, but I'm beginning to think that it won't be coming from me.

"Only once," he says tightly. "I've taken your memories only once."

"Tell me," I demand, though I am certain that I already know.

"Just a few days ago," he says. "You were chasing a cat."

I close my eyes. That was the day that I arrived in New York. Brayden and I were heading back to his apartment, and we saw his neighbor's cat. We chased Roger into an alley, but I'd thought we had too much to drink because after that the night was a blur, and I woke up in the guest bed feeling warm and wonderful in the aftermath of a truly exceptional erotic dream.

"You touched me," I accused. "You *fucked* me."

He flinches as if I have slapped him. "You remembered me. For the first time in three thousand years you looked in my eyes and you said my name. Christ, Christina, you wanted me as badly as I wanted you, and I couldn't wait. So god help me, but yes. Instead of killing you as I knew I should, I took you in a goddamn alley when you deserved so much better."

I feel a tear trickle down my cheek. "You took my memory. Of us."

"No—no." He is out of the chair immediately. "You'd already forgotten me." His voice softens with pain. "Once I pulled out your energy and brought the weapon down, you forgot everything."

I can hear the sadness in his voice, and I turn away, not sure if I want to hear what he has to say or if I want to run from it.

"I took the rest of your memories because Brayden was passed out and there was a headless woman on the ground who I was about to turn to dust. I couldn't have you seeing that. And I needed time to think. To figure out what—"

"*You* needed time?"

To his credit, he doesn't answer. Smart man.

I hold up a hand. "You know what? Right now, I need a little time."

"Christina—"

"Jaynie," I say firmly. "It's Jaynie. And don't push me. Don't make what's already hard even harder."

I GO INTO the first room I come to and call Brayden.

I'm not sure why—it's not like I can tell him what's bothering me without telling him everything. And even if I wanted to do that, I can hardly do it over the phone. The story of my life requires in person and alcohol. That's just a basic, fundamental truth.

But even if he doesn't know my secrets,

he's still my best friend, and I need to hear his voice. I need him to tell me that everything will be okay, even if he doesn't know what everything is.

He picks up on the second ring. "Hey," I say. "Where are you?" It occurs to me belatedly that he might be with Dagny. She's one of the female members of the brotherhood, and I vaguely remember her from my ancient past. Brayden doesn't know that, though. He thinks she's just a VIP at Dark Pleasures—and that she's a very hot woman with whom he hit it off.

"Just walked in," he says. "Where are you?"

"At Mal's." I keep my voice casual. No trouble here. Which, of course, entirely defeats the point of calling in the first place.

"I figured," he says. "I don't think I've ever seen you click with someone like that."

I don't answer. I'm pacing the room, not really seeing it. Just paying enough attention so that I don't bump into furniture. The huge modern desk, all chrome and glass.

The dark wooden bookcases. The giant abstract painting that I think is an original Jackson Pollock.

I turn away, intimidated by both the physical size and the price tag of the art.

"Jay?" Brayden presses. "Did I lose you?"

"Sorry. Bad connection. What?" I'm behind Mal's desk now, trailing my finger over the top of the credenza. And as I do, I cannot help but see the small section of the bookcase devoted to a collection of miniature picture frames.

"I said that you two clicked."

"Yeah." My voice sounds distracted even to my own ears. There's something so familiar about these photos. "Yeah," I repeat. "We really do. I—I guess I just wanted to hear that from you, too. You know me. Always needing validation."

"I do know you, and I think it's great. So long as you're not planning on fucking and running. I like Dagny. I don't want you to blow it for me by proxy."

I make a face at the phone, but I don't deny. That's my usual pattern, after all. Meet a guy. Fuck a guy. Leave a guy.

Because how can you trust a guy not to hurt you first?

The thought seems to twist around my heart. Because didn't Mal do exactly that?

He didn't. It's entirely different.

I frown and push down the voice in my head that is determined to be sensible and reasonable. "I'm glad you and Dagny are getting on. I figured you must be when Mal said he bribed you with her phone number."

"Let's just say I had a really great morning."

I laugh. "That's awesome."

"Jay?" His voice has turned serious. "Why did you really call? Is something the matter?"

I hesitate, but the truth is that although I want to hold tight to my anger, I know that it's not real. It's a knee-jerk reaction, because this is what I do. I make up excuses to run. Excuses not to get close.

But with Mal, my usual pattern isn't going to work.

And that's just a little terrifying.

And that, of course, is why I ran.

"Nothing's the matter," I tell Bray before the pause gets too long and he really does start to worry. "Just the opposite. In fact I was calling to tell you I'm staying here tonight. So don't worry, okay."

"You sure? That's awfully fast."

"I'm sure," I say, then promise to call him tomorrow.

I've idly opened a wooden box that sits on the shelf beneath the photographs. Inside, I find the resume I sent to Story Street when I signed up to audition for Juliet, along with my headshot. And beneath that are several other small items. Tiny paintings. Coins. A small cloth doll. Somehow, they are all familiar.

Atop them all is a small, yellowing sketch of a young woman with wild curls and penetrating eyes. The words on the bottom are in French, but I know what they say. *To remember me by when you cross the sea.*

The memory floods over me. I'd given it to my fiancé when he'd left Paris to come to America over two hundred years ago. His ship had been lost in a storm, and I had been lost in grief. I had not loved him—I had never loved any man—but I had been fond of him. And I'd wanted so desperately to leave France, which had always seemed to be a place full of danger, though in truth I knew that it was myself from whom I wished to run.

When the stranger came with his odd sword and took my life in that cold Parisian street, I did not flinch. Hadn't I always known that the end would come? One thing did surprise me—the words he spoke. "My love," he'd said in a language I did not then understand. "Please forgive me."

I had died only moments later, and only now does the memory of those words return to me.

Please forgive me.

Oh, dear god, I do understand why Mal

took my memories. I even know why he destroyed me over and over again.

And each time he cut me down, he destroyed himself, too. Only he didn't have my luxury of forgetting.

On the contrary, he kept these horrible souvenirs to remind him of what he had to do—and of what he'd lost so many times.

I had the luxury of oblivion.

He had the pain of loss.

The door opens, and I look up guiltily, realizing that I am still holding the French sketch. "You kept souvenirs," I say stupidly. "Doesn't that make it all worse?"

His smile barely touches his lips, but the sadness clings to him like a blanket. "There is no way it could be worse."

I put the sketch back in the box and go around the desk to face him. "I'm sorry I got mad."

"I'm sorry for so many things," he says. "Mostly I'm sorry I didn't protect you better all those years ago."

At his words, my heart melts a bit. "Do

you think I don't understand? I do." I reach out and touch his cheek. "I don't like it, but I understand that you did what you had to."

He just shakes his head, and he looks so wrecked it makes me want to cry. "We've lost so much. *Goddamn them.*" The curse seems ripped from him, and I look up, confused. "The fuerie," he explains. "Everything we had together, shattered in one night. One night when they took you from our camp and I wasn't there to protect you."

"You are always there, Mal. How could you be anywhere but with me?"

I mean the words with all my heart, but at the same time I know that will not help him. Not now. And so I go to him, succumbing to the passion that immediately sparks between us. It's passion and heat, yes. But it's also familiar. And even with the specter of the weapon hanging over us, I know that I am safe in his arms.

We've known each other for an eternity, and yet there are so many things that we have to rebuild. So much we still have to learn. But this is how we are connected— this is how we will move forward.

In touch and heat. In sex and submission. In passion and power, fire and desire.

They are keys for us. The way back to each other. The way to save the world.

"Kiss me," I beg. And when his mouth closes over mine, it feels like coming home.

CHAPTER 6

S INCE I DON'T have a change of clothes, I borrow a pair of sweatpants and a T-shirt from Mal. The pants swallow me, and I have to roll the waist band over about a dozen times. The T-shirt bears the logo for Phoenix Security and hangs down to just above my knees.

I'm standing in his stadium-sized bathroom studying my reflection in the mirror. The outfit may look ridiculous, but I can't deny that I like the way it feels to be wrapped up in his clothes like this. It's warm and casual and wonderful. And not just because I am practically vibrating with unfulfilled sexual potential.

Unfulfilled in that I successfully—though frustratingly—managed hold back a grand total of four orgasms that promised to be amazing. But that small blip in my personal satisfaction isn't a problem, but a victory.

No, this warm and fuzzy feeling stems not from orgasmic delight, but from the feeling of togetherness. A sense of rightness that comes from the man—from the two of us together—and not just from the knowledge that thousands of years ago we were bound. It's now. And it's right. And it's real.

And as I look in the mirror, I realize that I am smiling.

"You look like you're thinking deep, but happy thoughts," Mal says as he comes into the bathroom and stands behind me. He's dressed now in jeans and a black T-shirt and looks as sexy as sin. To be honest, I'm no slouch either. I'm reasonably tall, though Mal still towers over me, and I have the kind of wavy brown hair that stylists love because it always seems to cooperate. I inherited my oval-shaped face and big brown eyes from my mother, and they are an asset as an actress, because if nothing else I can always rock the headshot.

The truth is, we make an attractive couple, and as I look at our reflection, I cannot suppress a sigh of contentment. Because despite all the weirdness going on around me, being in Mal's arms feels right.

He puts his hands gently on my shoulders and bends down to press a kiss to the top of my head. "Will you tell me?"

I reach up and take his hands, then ease them down so that he is embracing me just below my breasts. "I was thinking how this moment feels so right. Comfortable and warm and, I don't know, *real*."

I shrug, because I know I'm not expressing myself very well, in part because I'm not ready to tell him everything about my life before. About how reality has always seemed a little skewed and overwhelming to me, partly because I've seen it through the eyes of my mother.

And how even though I know—I *know*—that everything that is happening with him is true and real and amazing and terrifying and so many other things, at the same time there is some tiny part of me that fears that it's all a delusion. Because while being in Mal's arms feels real, the memories that have been creeping back do not.

Mal, of course, knows none of my fears. But apparently he does know me, because he murmurs, "Well, this isn't fair. My pants and T-shirt made you happy, but now I've gone and done something to make you melancholy. Should I just go and leave you alone with my clothes?"

I shake my head, knowing that I should let him in, but unable to dredge up the words. I *do* trust him—and when I'm in his arms there is no denying the intensity of the connection between us.

So why the hell can I not tell him my fears?

"Hey, it's okay." His voice is soft, and he

turns me in his arms so that I am facing him. Then he lifts my chin and brushes a soft kiss over my lips. "You don't have to be scared."

I look up, wondering if he also has the power to read my mind. And then I think that maybe his real gift is the power to loosen my tongue, because suddenly it's all spilling out of me. "It's just—okay, it's these memories I'm getting back. They're like a dream. A nice dream, sure. But they don't feel real to me. They're like, I don't know, information that I read in a book. Interesting, but not a part of me."

Mal is looking at me as if what I have to say is the most important thing in the world, and that look of pure attention gives me the courage to go on.

"But you ..." I trail off, feeling a bit at loose ends, then move across the huge room to sit on a padded bench. "I met you and the world fell away. And when I see the way you look at me, it humbles me."

"All I'm seeing is the woman you are," he says, moving to sit on the edge of the tub near me.

"Are you? Because I worry that you're seeing a woman who I'm not even certain exists anymore." I think of all those things in his office. Souvenirs of my other lives—I don't even remember most of them. They have no meaning to me. But they do mean something to him.

"Oh, lover, no." He moves off the tub to kneel in front of me, and takes my hands in his, then brushes a gentle kiss over my knuckles. "You're my mate, Christina, and neither time nor distance nor death can change that."

I nod. In our original world, our dimension, the mating ritual formed a permanent melding of two life forces—energy—that even death could not break. And I know that by reminding me that we are mated, he is trying to soothe me, but his words have the opposite effect.

I tug my hands free and start to pace, because I'm too antsy to stay still. "There is a connection between us, and it is amazing and wonderful, and I do not deny it. But a few days ago I didn't know it existed. I didn't even know you existed. But you've had thousands of years to build this up in your mind. To fantasize about having Christina—having me—back in your arms. In your bed." I swallow and look down at the floor. "What if the woman you remember isn't the one who is here with you now?"

He stands as well, then takes my hand and tugs me to a stop. "This isn't a game or a passing fancy," he says. "We're connected, Jaynie," and his use of the name that I was given in this life brings tears to my eyes. "I feel it. And lover, I know that you do, too."

I realize that I am nodding, accepting and acknowledging that one basic truth.

"I'm willing to start there," he says simply. "To hold tight to this vibrant and beautiful woman who fills me. And I look forward to exploring her. To learning everything about her."

His eyes meet mine, and I see the passion of his words reflected back at me. "And lover, we have all the time in the world to know each other. Physically. Emotionally. Intimately."

He strokes my cheek, and it is only then that I realize that I am crying and that he is brushing away a tear. "Tell me you want that, too."

"Yes," I whisper, meaning it fully. He has, in that incredible way of his, managed to not only assuage my fears, but make me feel incredibly lucky that this man belongs to me.

But still a question lingers, and I have to ask it. "But do we, Mal? Do we really have all the time in the world?"

He cocks his head. "I'm immortal. Or hadn't you heard? I haven't aged a day in a very, very long time."

"You haven't," I say. "But I have."

I can tell by the way his face turns totally expressionless that this is not something he'd thought of. That amid the thrill and drama of both finding me and not killing me, the problem of what happens to me if I continue to live and breathe hadn't occurred to him.

And when he moves to sit on the tub again—when he draws a breath and says, "Oh, Christ," I know that I have actually managed to throw Malcolm Greer for a loop.

Somehow, that accomplishment doesn't make me proud.

"Why?" I ask. "Why do I age and you don't?"

He shakes his head. "The same reason your essence remains contained when you die. The same reason you die at all. The same reason that it is always you when you are reborn, fully and completely, even though the body is different." He looks up and faces me. "It's the weapon. Somehow, having the weapon inside you changes everything. We'll get it out, and you'll be as you were, okay?"

I nod, feeling just a little numb.

"Because I am not losing you again. Not ever."

"No," I whisper. "Not ever. But how? How will we get it out of me?"

He glances at the clock—it's almost four.

"That's what we're going to go see about now."

CHAPTER 7

THE DEBRIEF TAKES place in the private courtyard that connects Mal's brownstone to Number 36, and when we arrive, Jessica and Liam are both already there. She comes to me immediately, but Liam only nods, then signals for Mal to join him.

"Is the nod good or bad?" I ask Jessica, as I watch the two men. Mal, tall and lean, commanding and strong, with what I think is a truly exceptional ass filling out a pair of well-worn jeans. Liam, big enough to be a professional football player, with an air of power tempered by the kind of eyes that ensure that people not only trust him, but obey him.

"The nod is good," Jessica assures me. "It means you're not so much of a problem that he has to take the time to handle you."

"All right, then." I'm actually feeling a bit smug, but that fades when I see Asher step out of Number 36 to join us in the courtyard. He looks at Mal and Liam, then looks at me. And though I expect him to ignore me, he comes over.

"I should apologize for trying to kill you," he says, the formality of his words sounding very odd considering the subject matter.

"Oh." I have absolutely no clue how to respond.

"It was inappropriate of me, and I regret my decision to ignore not only the chain of command but a direct order."

"Um." I say, which is not a big improvement on my last remark.

"You should apologize," Jessica says. "You were an utter ass."

Ash inclines his head, his copper-colored

hair glinting in the lowering sun. "So Liam has told me." He shifts his attention back to me. "I also want to let you know that it's nothing personal. As I said before, I'm very fond of you, and always have been. But I think it's a mistake for you to be in corporeal form when you are playing host to the fuerie's weapon. And I want to apologize prospectively for arguing my position in that regard today."

I gape at him. "What the hell are you talking about?" Still not the most articulate of responses, but better than I've managed before.

"I'm going to tell Liam and Mal that I want them to rethink their position. You were attacked by the fuerie. There will be more attacks. You're a goddamn magnet, and while the upside might be that you draw them in and we take them out, I think we all know that the downside is significantly more severe."

"Goddamn it, Ash," Jessica says.

He holds his hands out, the picture of

politeness. "I'm just keeping Christina in the loop."

I want to bite out a sarcastic reply, but I can't manage to conjure the words. And so Ash just nods his head in a parting gesture and goes to join Liam and Mal.

I start to follow, but Jessica grabs my sleeve and pulls me back. "Mal won't change his mind, and nothing Ash can say right now can change Liam's. Let them be. Really."

"Nothing he can say right now?" I repeat.

Jessica lifts a shoulder. "You're a risk— we all know it. But Mal talked to Liam and told him you two are working hard on your control." She shrugs and I try very hard not to look mortified as I hope and pray that Mal didn't tell Liam *how* exactly we were working on that.

"Right now, the risk is minimal," Jessica continues smoothly. "And the truth is, everyone wants you here."

I frown. "Everyone but Asher."

Jessica's mouth pulls into a thin line.

"Yeah, well, he's a little conflicted. He does like you—you remember you two were good friends?"

"I believe you," I say. "But no, I don't really remember."

"Well, you were. Oh, hell, we all were. But what happened in Alexandria hurt Ash the most."

"Alexandria?"

Her eyes widen, and then she closes them as she takes a deep breath. "Shit. You don't remember."

"What happened?" I hear the urgency in my voice.

For a moment, I think she won't answer. "You almost went nuclear," she finally says. "Mal got to you before it got completely out of control, but it was bad. And a woman Asher cared for—"

"She died." My voice is flat. Numb.

Jessica doesn't reply. She just pulls me into a quick, awkward hug. "I've missed you, Christina," she says when we pull apart. "And don't worry. We all understand that it's not your fault. And we get that you don't remember everything yet, too. But we were friends back in the day. I hope we will be again."

"So do I," I say, and I really mean it.

A moment later, she raises her hand to motion someone over, and I turn to see Dagny approaching with a curvy blonde. They're both casual—Dagny wears a pair of paint-stained yoga pants and her auburn curls are piled on top of her head and held in place with a chopstick. The blonde is in jeans and a law school T-shirt, with her hair pulled back into a ponytail.

"Christina," Dagny says. "It's great to see you again."

"You, too," I say, feeling a little weird. I'd had no idea who I was—or what she was—when we met in Dark Pleasures Saturday night. "Did you just come from Brayden's?"

"Yup. He says hi."

"You told him you were coming here?"

"Sure—oh, I haven't told him everything. Just that I had an owners' meeting and that Mal would be there and that probably meant that you would, too."

"I'm glad it's going well," I say, and though I mean it, I'm also worried about the secrets. And about Bray getting hurt.

"He's really great," Dagny says. "The truth is, I gave up dating a long time ago. Too painful." She lifts a shoulder in a tiny shrug. "But Brayden makes me want to dive back into the pool."

"What do you mean?"

There's no time for her to answer, though, because the blonde approaches and holds out her hand to me. "I'm Callie. I'm with Raine." She glances around. "Well, not at this particular moment, but you know what I mean."

I laugh, because I do. "I'm with Mal."

"Don't anyone say anything interesting until I get back," Dagny says. "I'm starving." She moves over to where a spread of light snacks is set out on a table on the far side of the courtyard.

"She can eat anything and not gain an ounce," Callie says, then grins. "Bitch."

I laugh. "So, um, Raine," I say to Callie. "I remember him, I think. But I can't picture him."

"He looks a lot different than when you knew him," Jessica says. "He's pretty much covered in tats these days."

I remember the man with the tattoos who'd been sitting next to Malcolm when I first saw him at Dark Pleasures. "Tats? From the phoenix fire?"

Callie nods.

"How many times has he—"

"Too many," Callie says sharply, and I realize that I have hit on a sore point.

"Raine's close to the hollow," Jessica says, and though I can tell from her voice that it's serious, I don't know what that means.

Jessica sees my confusion and exhales. "We're immortal," she says. "But that refers to the body. Too many times into the burn and, well, it hollows you right out. Raine was reckless for years and now he's close. If he dies again, he may not come back even when he comes back."

"I'm sorry," I say, as Callie shoves her hands in her pockets and looks at the ground.

I clear my throat. "So, I think I do remember Raine, at least a little. But I don't remember you at all," I say to Callie.

She lifts her head to look at me, and I think that she's grateful for the change in subject. "We kind of knew each other back in the day, but I wouldn't look familiar to you."

"Kind of?" I ask, as I take a tiny sandwich off the plate that Dagny has returned with.

"Livia," Dagny says. "Part of Livia's essence is inside Callie."

"Livia?" My memory is like an unfinished jigsaw puzzle with several pieces still missing. But the piece with Livia is there, and I shake my head in wonder. "But I thought Livia was thrust back into the void."

"So did Raine," Callie says.

"So did everyone," Jessica clarifies. "Turns out her essence remained and ended up twined with a human's, but not melding the way we did. The human died, her essence got diluted. And on and on. A lot of time. A lot of births. A lot of lives. But at the core, some of Livia still remains."

I frown, because I know that I am not like that. I'm entirely me, one-hundred percent undiluted Christina.

And all because of the weapon.

I'm about to ask another question when I hear Dante's voice over the general hum of conversation. "Sorry! Raine and I got tied up on Skype with Trace. Didn't mean to keep everyone waiting."

"It's fine," Liam says. "But let's begin. Everyone take a seat."

There is a large rectangular table over to one side of the courtyard, and as the group heads that direction, I hang back, intending to sit in one of the lounge chairs and just listen. Mal, however, puts a quick stop to that plan. "With me," he says. "You are entitled to a place at the table as much as any of us."

"Am I?" I can't help glancing toward Asher as I speak.

"Yes," he says firmly. "You are."

I consider arguing—telling him that I'd be more comfortable hanging back and just soaking it all in—but I realize that he and Liam have both stood up for me. Not just because I am Mal's mate, but because what and who I am ensures my place in the brotherhood. So, yes, I will sit at the table.

Mal pulls out a chair for me between Raine and Jessica, but he sits at one end of the table while Liam sits at the other.

Liam calls the meeting to order, then asks Dante to give his report.

"I've checked in with all the field offices," he says. "No surprises. Trace reports that the London office took out two more fuerie in the last week. Paris is still running hot. Rachel tells me the terrorist bomb threats are continuing, but her team has managed to take out three of the bombers and foil four attacks, so I'd say it's under control even though it's not yet resolved."

He continues to run through a list of foreign offices, then looks at Dagny, silently giving her the floor.

"Smith tells me he's up to speed on Los Angeles, so I guess that makes me a permanent New Yorker now," she says. "And I've checked in with Chicago, Dallas and Seattle. Nothing out of the ordinary."

"And here?" Mal asks, looking to Dante once again. "Have you sensed any fuerie around our perimeter?" He shifts his attention to me, and I understand what he is asking: *Is anyone coming after Christina?*

Dante shakes his head. "Nothing. But we all know my range is limited. They could be out there, just keeping to a wide perimeter."

"All right," Mal says. "Then let's move on to Phoenix Security. What have we heard from Munich and the Liesl Albrecht kidnapping?"

"Wait," I say, and everyone turns to me.

I'm not exactly sure what I mean to ask, and I look to Mal for help. He leans forward, clearly about to speak, but Liam does so first.

"Apologies, Christina. It's unfair to have you at the table and yet not have you fully briefed." He glances at everyone. "Any objections to taking a few moments to catch Christina up?"

No one objects. From the tone of Liam's voice, it is clear that it wasn't really an open offer.

"You're aware of our primary mission?"

"Of course," I say. "To capture and render the fuerie inert." I don't say kill, since the fuerie is a malevolent energy, and energy can be neither created nor destroyed.

When we set off on our mission to regain the weapon and stop the fuerie, we were tasked with trapping the fuerie's energy and either returning it to our world so that it could be bound in a containment cell for eternity or thrusting it into the netherworld between dimensions. Essentially imprisoning it there where it could do no harm. Not death, but as close as could be achieved for a creature of pure energy.

I say all that at the table, and am impressed with myself by how much of my memory returns simply as I talk about it. I glance at Mal when I'm finished and am warmed by his small nod of approval.

"And here? In this world? Do you know how the fuerie manifests?"

This question is trickier, because my memory is very limited. "I've seen them here," I say. "In New York. They appear human, but to me—to us—their faces look to be made of flame." I glance around the table. "But they're not like the brotherhood. No human willingly let the fuerie in. It's like possession. Like *The Exorcist*," I add, referring to the horror movie that had completely creeped me out when I saw it as a child.

"For that matter, if we're going with pop culture references, the fuerie is kind of like the Borg." I had been a fan of all things *Star Trek* growing up. "It's one entity—one sentient consciousness. But it gets broken up into parts, and those parts live in a whole bunch of humans."

Beside me, Raine nods, and I have to fight a grin, feeling a bit like a prized pupil.

Liam's expression doesn't change, but I think that I see approval in his eyes as well, though that might just be wishful thinking.

"And our mission? As the brother-hood?"

I hesitate, thinking this must be a trick question. "Um, kill the fuerie?" I frown a bit, thinking of Linda Blair as poor little Regan, all full up with the demon. "But doesn't that kill the human, too?"

"A human possessed by a fuerie is al-ready dead," Jessica says flatly. "The fuerie's energy burns them out within minutes."

"Oh." I shiver. "And when we kill the fuerie?" I can picture Mal and Dante fighting in that alley. The fuerie falling, then turning to dust when stabbed through the heart.

"Their energy returns to the fabric of this dimension," Asher says. "But what do we know about this dimension?"

I shift in my chair like an unprepared student taking an oral exam. But I soldier on. "In this world, sentient energy must be contained in a vessel."

"Right," Jessica says. "So if we kill the fuerie and there is no human nearby into which it can get a foothold, then that energy is absorbed into fabric of the universe. And the consciousness of the fuerie as a whole is reduced by that much."

"That's good, though, right?"

"It's very good," Liam says. "But we have been undertaking this task for three thousand years now, and the fuerie is still strong, despite having felled thousands of its foot soldiers. And the truth is that some of those who work with the fuerie are simply human."

I frown, not understanding.

"Think of the most evil people in history," Mal explains. "Most likely those people were of the fuerie. They often manifest as charming. Personable. Intelligent. And they rally humans to follow them. Hitler was of the fuerie. So was Ted Bundy."

Across the table from me, Dante shrugs. "The fuerie didn't bring evil to this world. It just added to it."

My head is spinning, but I think I understand. "And Phoenix Security?"

"We formed it centuries ago, though the name has changed over time." Mal is leaning back in his chair, looking at me as he speaks. "The idea was to have a sort of front company. A detective agency. Bodyguards. Whatever best suited our needs. And we used the resources of that company to track down and destroy the fuerie."

"That's evolved, though," Raine says. "Over half our business now has nothing to do with the fuerie. We offer protection services, find missing children, stop assassins, investigate serial killers, and even have the ear of a number of political leaders and investigative agencies around the globe. I was about to report on little Liesl, and I'm happy to say that the German team reports that we not only recovered her safe and healthy, but also delivered her kidnappers to the Munich authorities. Needless to say, the work is rewarding."

"And being immortal provides us with an interesting perspective on the world," Dante adds. "And our resources—including our finances—are essentially unlimited."

"And the wider our base," Liam concludes, "the more it benefits the dual mission of seeking out and destroying the fuerie."

"That's a mission that could take forever," I say.

"Eventually we'll prevail." Mal looks at everyone at the table. "That is why we were given the gift of immortality, after all."

Beside me, Raine shifts as if uncomfortable, but when I look at him, his eyes are fixed on Mal.

"But with luck and diligence," Mal continues, "the fuerie's defeat will not take that long. Soon, we hope to bind it in its entirety."

"How?"

"The amulets," Callie tells me.

"There are seven amulets," Raine explains. "We have six. Once we have the seventh in our possession, we can bind the fuerie, then send it into the void. Or even back to our world so that it can be bound in a containment center."

"And Christina…" Mal's voice is gentle, and I turn from Raine to face him. "Together, the seven amulets can withdraw and contain the weapon inside you."

A shiver cuts through me. "Where is it?" I'm almost afraid to ask. The thought that something out there in the world could set me free of this weapon is almost too much to believe. "Where's the seventh amulet?"

Raine and Callie exchange a look. "Lost," Callie says. "My father found it. He didn't know what he'd found, but … well, anyway, it's lost again."

"And Phoenix Security is investigating that theft as well," Liam says. "Any leads on identifying the fuerie who ran off with it?"

"Not yet," Raine says. "The security cameras in the shop didn't have a good angle. But there were some reflective surfaces and I'm talking to the computer, hoping to convince it to do some magic with the pixels."

"Raine's good with computers," Jessica whispers. "Just like I'm good with healing."

I nod, but I'm not really listening. I can't stop thinking about that seventh amulet.

Find it, and I'm free.

Find it, and I'll be whole.

I glance toward Mal only to see that he is already looking at me.

Yes.

He mouths the word and nothing else. But that is enough. It's a promise, and I cling to it.

We will find the amulet.

We will save me.

And in that moment, my worries fade away. Because I trust him. And though I do not know how he will manage it, I know that is a promise that he will keep.

CHAPTER 8

AFTER THE MEETING, I borrow a skirt and blouse from Callie, then hang out with the girls in the members area at Dark Pleasures.

"The VIP room is the place if we want to just kick back," Jessica says as the waiter brings us each a glass of scotch. "But for people watching and catching up on gossip, it's way more fun in here."

She's right, and while we sip scotch and chat about everything from the various jobs of the members who are scattered about—including two actors I recognize from a recent run on Broadway—to our own careers, I can't help but think how nice it is to just sit and talk with other women. Jessica is smart and funny and really did go to med school. Harvard, actually, class of 1945. The very first year that Harvard Medical School admitted women.

"I'd been a healer before that," she says. "But for a long time I was considered a charmer or even a witch." She shrugs. "Those were fun times. Not."

"Jessica was actually burned at the stake once," Dagny says, to which Callie and I reply in unison, "Seriously?"

Jessica nods. "Laying low is not my strong suit. Drives Liam crazy."

"The hell it does," Dagny counters. "Like he'd want a woman who's quiet and demur."

Jessica's brows rise just slightly. "Are you suggesting I'm not demur?" she asks, and we all laugh.

"I know Callie's a lawyer," I say to Dagny. "But what do you do? Other than Phoenix Security, I mean."

"That's it," she says. "But it's more than

you think." Her smile is thin and very smug. "A few of us—including Mal and Raine, by the way—have put in time with various intelligence agencies. Honing our skills, you know. I've worked at the CIA, done a stint at ATF, did the Pinkertons thing for a while, but back then I had to be the office girl. And," she adds, falling into a British accent, "I put in a full ten years with MI-6."

I glance at Callie. "Did you know that?"

"Not a clue." She narrows her eyes at Dagny. "How do you deal with the background checks?"

"Oh, please. You live long enough you figure out how to do all sorts of things. Not to mention, these days people believe anything that's in their database. And Raine can fix any database to match any situation."

I sit back and finish my scotch, astounded by the world I've fallen into. "It's amazing."

"What is?" Dagny asks.

"This. You guys. Well, us." I frown, because I'm a part of this too, now. "It's the stuff of fantasies. Or psychoses," I add sardonically.

"You're not crazy, Christina," Jessica says, and her voice and smile are so soft and gentle that I can't help but wonder if she knows about my mother. Even as the thought enters my head, I realize that she must. Because Jessica is a doctor, and as far as she's concerned, I'm her patient, and she would have gone out of her way to find out everything she can about me.

Surprisingly, the thought doesn't piss me off. In fact, it's strangely comforting.

We stay like that, talking and laughing, for a few more hours and a few more drinks, and I am grateful that I only have to cross the courtyard to get home. "And you're close, too," I say to Callie, who I happen to know lives in the fabulous penthouse apartment of Number 36.

"I am," she says. "And if you need more clothes for tomorrow, just let me know."

"Thanks," I say, though I really need to get back to Brayden's and pack a bag.

"I'm in the Village," Jessica says. "But Liam's with Dante over in the VIP lounge, so I'll cut out when he's ready."

"And you?" I ask Dagny, who immediately turns pink. I burst out laughing. "You aren't!"

She nods. "I told Brayden I'd come over when I was through, no matter how late."

"Do you want my key?"

Surprisingly, her blush actually deepens. "Actually, he already gave me one."

I meet Callie's eyes and we share a smile.

And then I leave my new girlfriends and stumble out of the members' area and through the private door into the lobby that was a grand ballroom before this building was converted. I cross the courtyard and let myself into Mal's building.

I pause just inside the door and breathe deep, wondering at the simple, basic, undeniable fact that it feels as though I belong here. That this place that I barely know already seems like home.

I wait for that realization to scare me.

And instead, I find myself smiling.

I take the stairs up to the den, then find Mal in his office.

He's bent over his laptop and is cursing like a sailor, pissed off that the goddamned motherfucking machine keeps fucking crashing.

I can't help it. I lean against the door-jamb and laugh.

Mal looks up, his expression irritated at first, but that fades to a resigned amusement when he realizes it's me.

"Shall I call Raine over?" I ask. "Maybe he could talk some sense into the mother-fucking machine."

He lifts one brow in a way that I consider desperately sexy. "Careful," he says in a voice that is so full of heat I swear the only reason I don't come right then is that I am not allowed to. "Keep talking sass and I may have to turn you over my knee."

"Oh, no you don't," I say, forcing myself not to laugh. But then I squeal when he comes around the desk. I run into the den with Mal right behind me, but I'm not trying too hard to get away. And when he does catch me, I can't deny that I'm kind of hoping he does exactly what he has threatened.

The thing is, that's not something I've done in bed, and I've never fantasized about being spanked. But there was something so enticing about the way he said it. And this game that we've been playing—if you can even call it a game when the fate of the world depends on my sexual responsiveness and control—has made me realize that there is a lot of untapped sexual potential out there in the world, and I want to push a few more boundaries. At least so long as it's Mal that I'm pushing against.

I don't, however, have the guts to ask for it.

Not that I have time to think about this perceived vacancy in our sex life. My mind is too full of him. The way he's pulling me close. The way his mouth closes over mine.

I moan softly and press against him, and

just like that all the playfulness between us evaporates, replaced by heat and passion and an almost violent need.

"Strip," he says as soon as he breaks the kiss. "I want to see you naked."

I don't hesitate. I'd borrowed a simple silk tank from Callie and paired it with a flowy maxi-skirt, and a pair of three-inch heels. I don't have a sister, but if I had, I would have wanted her closet to be much like Callie's.

I pull the tank over my head and toss it at Mal, who catches it, balls the material, then presses his face against it. "Lover, you smell like sin."

There's something so sensual about his words that I add an extra shimmy as I peel the skirt down over my hips, then let it fall in a puddle around my feet. I carefully step out of the ring of material, a move that puts me a good eight inches closer to Mal.

And even in that small distance, I can feel the increase in the tension between us.

I stand still for a moment, my legs slightly parted, my hip cocked just a bit. I am wearing Callie's three-inch heels, my own plain cotton bra, and no panties since I have no spare and Mal already destroyed the ones I'd arrived in.

Mal's eyes take it all in, his heated gaze moving so slowly over me that I am fairly certain he is actually touching me. And when his inspection finally ceases at my toes, I am so wet and ready that my sex is actually throbbing with need.

"Please," I say, and am rewarded with a slow, sexy smile that practically drips with promise.

"The rest," he orders, and I obey immediately so that I am entirely naked.

He nods toward the bedroom. "On the bed. Legs spread. Touch yourself," he demands. "But remember—you can't come."

"Wait—what?" I've gotten myself off before, of course. But never when a guy was around. And certainly not with one watching.

But all he does is press his fingertip to my lips and say, "Now."

I go. Because this is the plan. This is the game. This back and forth of control and submission is how I am learning to keep a rein on the wildness inside me.

That is the reason, of course.

But there is another reason, too. Because the idea of Mal watching as I touch myself is undeniably exciting. And as I spread out on the bed—as I slide my hand between my legs—I imagine that it is Mal touching me. Mal's mouth upon me. Mal's cock thrusting inside me.

I am not usually one for fantasy when I masturbate, but I cannot deny that I am enjoying this. Hell, I'm getting into it. I keep my eyes closed and tease my clit with my fingers, so slick with my own arousal. I lift my hips and slide two fingers inside, moving in tandem with his imaginary thrusts. And I'm close, so close, and as I bite down on my lower lip and force my hand to slow, it is Mal's voice I imagine I hear—*That's it, lover.*

Close, and then back it off. Right to the peak, and then push it back down.

My eyes flutter open, and I realize that the voice wasn't just in my head. The man himself is right there, naked now and desperately hard—and my entire body flushes with the heat of a blush that starts at my toes and travels all the way up to my hairline.

"No," he says, moving to the edge of the bed and gently taking the hand that is now laying limp between my legs. "Don't you even think about being embarrassed. You're beautiful and hot and sexy, and I don't know when I have been so turned on."

I know that he has slept with a lot of women—a man like Mal, how could he not?—but with those words, he makes me believe what he has been telling me in so many ways. That I am his. And that we fit.

I am so lost in this sensual haze that I do not realize what he's doing until my arm is outstretched above my head. "Mal?"

I give my arm a tug, and it doesn't move.

He's very efficiently attached me to the headboard.

"What are you doing?"

He moves around the bed, brushing his hand over my naked body as he walks. "Tying you up."

"Oh."

Who knew that three tiny words could be so intoxicating, but they are. My nipples have hardened and I am even wetter than before, my sex clenching with need.

And because I am naked and spread-eagled on the bed, Mal sees it all. And he smiles.

I take my free hand and put it over my face, making him chuckle softly. "No," he says as he lifts that hand and repeats the process with the other bedpost. "Don't hide from me. Don't you know that seeing you excited gets me hard? Don't you know that right now, I don't want anything in this world except to be inside you?"

I know I should answer. Speak. Nod. Something.

But all I can manage is to breathe.

And then he moves on to my legs.

Oh sweet god.

In no time at all he has bound my legs to the two posts of the footboard, so that I am spread wide.

"Mal..." His name is a moan. A plea.

"Do you know why I want you like this?" he asks, his voice low and so edgy I think that he could cut me with his words.

"Tell me."

He slides his hands up my legs, moving so slowly it almost causes me physical pain. I buck, my hips rising and falling in anticipation, knowing the touch that is coming. Waiting for it. Wanting it.

"Because you can't get away from it."

"What?" My word is a whisper. A breath. He is so close to my sex, and I want to feel him there. I am right on the verge of coming—and the sensation is somehow more exquisite since I know that I can't go over into that chasm.

"Pleasure," he says, then moves his

hands away from my sex toward my hips. He slides up, stroking my waist, my breasts, then leans in so that his mouth brushes my ear. "Tied up like this you can't shift. You can't move. You can't escape the pleasure. You simply have to endure it, letting it fill you. Letting it become so potent it is almost pain. And then—my sweet Christina—you have to fight it back and swallow your own release."

I whimper.

I actually, seriously whimper.

"Too much?" he asks. "Shall I go?"

I meet his eyes. "Don't you dare."

His gray eyes are as hard as steel and so full of desire that I am almost afraid of what will happen when he touches me again. Will either of us be able to hold back? And if we destroy the world, will we even care?

"*Christina.*"

There is pain in his voice, and when he closes his hands over my breasts—when he bites and licks and teases his way down my belly until his mouth closes hot and hard and demanding over my cunt—I cry out with him, because I want everything he has to give, and we are both being punished. We are both victims of the fuerie. We are both desperately craving something we can't have and so wildness and passion is the only substitute for a dual explosion that—one day—I desperately hope we can share.

His tongue is inside me, and he is right—I have no defense against the onslaught of pleasure. And yet I have to defend myself. I have to fight these rising sensations even as I want more—so, so much more.

"Please," I beg, shifting my hips so that he lifts his head to look at me. I tilt my head up so that I can meet his eyes. "I want you inside me. Please—please. If you can't give me an orgasm, at least give me that."

He cocks a single brow, and I think my heart skips a little. "Lover, if that will help you out, I am happy to oblige."

I start to laugh, but it quickly turns to a moan as he slides up my body. He touches me all over, teasing with lips and fingers, his cock rubbing my skin as he moves his body so sweetly over my trapped form.

And then, oh yes, he is there. His cock thrusting inside me. Just a bit, just enough to make me crave more. To make me cry out with harsh demand, "Dammit, Mal, please, now. Please, just fuck me hard."

He does.

Oh, sweet heaven, he thrusts inside me hard and fast, and I feel so wonderfully, fabulously full. "Yes," I cry. "Oh, yes, please. I want to feel you explode inside me. Mal, please. Please let me feel you come. Now—oh, god, now before I get to close."

"Christina—"

My name is a groan, and as his body tightens then releases, I cry out in defense against the power that is rising within me.

"*No.*" I twist on the bed. "*No, no, no.*"

"Do you—"

"I'm okay." My reply is a shout, and I breathe hard. *I have this. I can do this.* I can fight down this need. This power. This explosion.

And then, miraculously, I start to settle. I breathe deep and close my eyes, and as I do Mal moves off me. I feel his lips brush over mine, then the delicious pressure of his body against mine.

"I did it," I say.

"You most certainly did."

I open my eyes and turn my head toward him. "You did it, too."

"Oh, yes," he says playfully, then kisses me. "You are exceptional." He sits up, then strokes his hands lazily over my arms. "Very exceptional."

He unties the bands that hold me to the bed. He repeats the process with my ankles, then settles next to me as he continues to stroke me lightly. "Bothering you?"

"You're very cruel," I say as a small shiver cuts through me. "But I have to confess I like it."

"Good to know." He brushes his lips over mine. "I also know that you're getting good at this. At keeping control. Holding back. We may have to step it up a notch. Truly test your boundaries."

"Okay," I say, and my voice comes out more breathy than I intend.

Mal's smile is both knowing and indulgent. "Something on your mind? Something that you want?"

I think of how I'd imagined the sting of his palm against my ass. But I can't bring myself to say it, and I don't understand why.

I trust this man—I do. So why can't I make the words come?

I don't know, but what I do say is the truth as well. "Only you." I snuggle close. "All I want is you."

CHAPTER 9

I WAKE WITH the sun, then creep out of bed and pad barefoot into the kitchen. I actually manage to make breakfast, which consists of finding frozen waffles in his freezer, toasting them, and pouring orange juice. I add a cup of coffee and call it a job well done.

I deliver it in bed and hope that he sees it for what it is—my way of saying that I love him, even though I can't say that I love him. Because while the Christina part of me is hopelessly, desperately, passionately in love with this man, the Jaynie part of me has protected her heart for too long, and those three little words are among the most terrifying in the universe. Especially since we are moving so fast—even though thousands of years isn't really fast at all.

His eyes open when I wave the coffee cup under his nose, and he smiles at me. "Nice way to wake up," he says, then slides up in bed so that I can put the tray on his lap.

"I would have done it up bigger, but I figured you'd get a little miffed if I went outside without a bodyguard." I may not like it, but I get it. The bad guys are after me, and that means I have to be careful. If nothing else, the nasty little attack and quite painful lashing across the chest taught me that.

"You figured right," he says. "And this breakfast couldn't be more perfect."

For that matter, our entire morning couldn't be more perfect. Mal has some work to catch up on, but he does it on his laptop while I study my lines. That's one of the nice things about performing in a Shakespeare play; it's very easy to find a copy of the script if you've left your pages behind.

When Mal's frustration with his computer gets to be too much, he runs lines with me, with him taking the role of Romeo. The irony of the two of us reading the lines of the star-crossed lovers is definitely not lost on me, and I can only hope that our own romance doesn't turn out to be a tragedy.

I'm about to say as much to him when my cell phone rings. The caller ID shows that it's Eric, my director, and I take the call, only to be disappointed to learn that he has to go to LA for a few days, which means no rehearsals for the first half of this week. "But I want everyone off book when I get back. And check your email," he adds. "My assistant's going to be sending you a schedule. Come in during your assigned time and meet with Jefferson about your costume and Marisol about your make-up. Got it?"

"Got it," I say, and when the call ends, I meet Mal's eyes. "No rehearsal."

"I heard. I think I should take you out

for a proper date."

"Really?"

"I told you, this is our time to get to know each other again."

His words make me feel warm. Cozy. And a little bit cherished.

We end up having sushi nearby then taking a cab to the theater. The show is spectacular, and I force Mal to hang around the stage door afterwards. Not because I want to get the actors' autographs, but because I just want to watch and imagine that one day that will be me.

Will it? Can it?

I turn to Mal, suddenly afraid. "I don't want to give up acting."

The weapon, the brotherhood, even Mal. They're all pressing down on me. Claiming and controlling me in ways that I didn't ask for and am not sure that I want. I feel bubbles of panic rise within me, and I reach out, clinging to Mal before the rising fear turns into something more dangerous.

I see the furrows on his brow as he

looks at me with genuine confusion. "Why would you give it up?"

I am swept away by such a wave of relief that I laugh out loud. "I don't know. I don't—"

He pulls me close and kisses me hard. "I don't want to change you, lover," he says, gently cupping my face in his hand. "I want to save you."

The words bring tears to my eyes. And though I know he is talking about the weapon, I can't help but think that Mal is saving me in so many ways, because even though my world seems to be changing and shifting with every step I take, I have never in my life felt so steady.

And just like that, I realize that I have to tell him all of it.

"I'm scared," I say.

He strokes my hair. "I know. But we'll get the weapon out. We'll get past this."

"No. Not about the weapon. Well, yes," I amend. "Of course I'm scared of the weapon, but that's not what I'm talking about."

"Then what?" he says gently.

I draw in a breath, then take his hand. We walk away from Times Square and the after-theater crowd. I have no destination in mind; I just need to move. "I feel like I'm living two lives. Jaynie. Christina."

"You are," he says. "This is all new, lover. It's going to take some time to get used to. Callie's making the adjustment," he adds. "Maybe you should talk to her? And there are a few others—Anya in Prague. Daniel in Chicago."

"It's not the same."

"No," he agrees. "With Callie and the others, they have only part of the original essence, and it's buried deep. Crew members we lost during the accident. You're unique— you remain entirely you. And you have a number of your memories back, and the rest will return in time."

"Yes," I say. "But that's not what I mean. Not entirely." I draw in a breath. "My mother was insane. I mean that literally."

He's stopped walking, and now he's watching my face. I don't see surprise, and again I wonder how much the brotherhood has dug up on me. I don't ask, though. No matter what he knows about my mother, he doesn't know how her problems make me feel. How they scare me.

And so I continue on.

"She used to just check out. She'd have these periods that she called gray moments. And she'd tell me I had the devil inside me. It's like on some level she knew the truth about me and she couldn't handle it."

"You don't have the devil inside you."

"No, but I do have the weapon. And I think I might have some of my mother inside me, too."

He is still watching me, but he says nothing, and so I start walking again, because I just need to move. "I'm afraid I can't handle it. That I'm as weak as she was. That reality—especially a reality as strange as this one—isn't something I'm strong enough to handle."

"You can," he says.

"How do you know?"

He pulls me to a stop and brushes a kiss over my lips. "Because I've seen your strength, Jaynie Christina Hart. I've watched you process and handle and adjust to a new reality where a weaker woman would have simply melted down. And I know because if it ever truly does get to be too much for you, then you have my strength to draw on, too. And I promise you—together we can handle anything."

"I—" I close my mouth, not sure what I wanted to say. Though that is a lie. I want to tell him I love him. But somehow I can't get those particular words to come. I tell myself that's okay. As Mal said, everything has been moving so fast. And it's hard to reconcile the girl I used to be—a girl who wouldn't even get close much less fall in love—with the woman who loves him.

So I say the only thing I can right now. I say, "Thank you."

And when he smiles, I know that I've

said the right thing.

We walk in comfortable silence for a few more blocks, then stop into a diner for late-night sandwiches and dessert and coffee. We end up talking and laughing until well past three in the morning, and when we finally roll back onto the street, Mal pulls out his cell phone.

"Who can you possibly be calling at three?"

"Dennis," he says. "We'll never get a cab at this hour."

I cock my head. "And so you're going to wake your driver? We can walk."

He studies me for a moment, then focuses on the strappy sandals I've borrowed from Callie.

"What? I can handle it. Besides, it's a fabulous night. And how often do we have the city almost all to ourselves?"

He nods in acquiescence then links his arm with mine. "You've convinced me," he says as we set off.

I'm right about it being a pleasant night,

and despite the hour, I'm not tired. Instead, I'm enjoying being with Mal. Hell, he energizes me even when he's not pouring energy back into me.

I'm just about to tell him that we should make a habit of taking long walks back from the theater when Mal stops.

"What?" I ask, but the word is barely out of my mouth before I realize that his fire sword is out and extended.

And that there are a grand total of six fuerie on the sidewalk with us—and they have us completely surrounded.

CHAPTER 10

"*DOWN!*"

Mal shouts the word even as he pushes me down with one hand. With the other, he lashes out with the fire sword, sending the blade of light swinging out in an arc around him.

I want to rise and help, but I am trapped. Terrified of these human-looking creatures who are looking at me. Lunging toward me. Kept away only by Mal's fire sword and his determination.

Two of the fuerie burst forward, a third protected between them.

The third lashes out with its whip, and I cry out in fear, unable from my prone position to even get out of the way.

But in a heartbeat, Mal is in front of the whip, and I suck in air, knowing too well the pain that he will feel.

The weapon only slices his jacket, though, and I am still gasping with relief when he is back in attack mode, a wild thing of fight and motion. Strong and powerful, a man possessed. A man who has the strength to protect me, just as he promised.

It is all over in seconds, and as Mal thrusts his fire sword through the hearts of the fallen fuerie, I realize that I am shaking and crying.

"Hey," he says soothingly as he crouches in front of me. "It's okay. You're safe. You're fine."

I shake my head, because it isn't only fear that has me blubbering.

Mal doesn't know that, though, and so he scoops me into his arms and carries me two blocks to a hotel where we are assured of getting a taxi.

I am still feeling numb when we enter

his brownstone and he carries me up the steps to the den.

"It's okay," he says. "You're safe. We're safe."

"No," I say. "No, goddammit, no." I shift in his arms, thrashing until he puts me down, then stares warily at me, as if I am something wild and about to attack.

Wise man, because that's pretty much the way I feel.

"I used to be a warrior." I practically spit the words. "I may not remember everything, but I remember that. I was a soldier, and I fought those creatures. That's why I was on the mission in the first place." The memories flood back over me even as I'm speaking, filling in the gaps in my memory. "Hell, I was on Liam's squad. One of the elite fighters. I wasn't a tech or support or in charge of goddamn requisitions. I was a fucking *fighter.*"

I run my fingers through my hair as I pace the room. "Now I can't even get into it with them, because I'm the goddamn prize in the cereal box. Because if I fight I might lose control. Hell, I might turn into fucking Hiroshima."

"Hey," he says gently. "It's okay."

"The hell it is." I'm standing by the wall, and I reach out and grab his collar and yank him toward me. "I don't even know what I am anymore."

For a moment, I think I see pain in his eyes, but I ignore it and burst forward, closing my mouth over his. Tasting him. *Taking* him.

With a violent motion, I shift our positions so that his back is against the wall and I am pressed against him. I feel his hesitation, as if sex with the pissed off crazy woman might not be such a great idea, but I am relentless, my mouth on his, my tongue tasting him, my hands ripping his shirt open with such wild abandon that the buttons go flying.

"You're still a fighter," he tells me, which at the moment is appropriate since I am attacking him. "You're just doing it differently now."

"Shut up, Mal," I demand. I don't know if it's fear from the attack or frustration from not being able to fight or lingering sexual frustration from my control sessions with Mal. But right then, the only thing in the world I care about is getting this man inside me. And I am relentless.

And thank god, so is he.

He grabs my ass and lifts me, and I hook my legs around his waist. He whips us around, so that now it is my back against the wall, and I am trapped between the hard plaster and the hard heat of his body.

With me stuck fast that way, he uses one hand to lower his fly, then shoves the skirt I borrowed from Callie up my thighs. I'm not wearing underwear, and when his fingers discover that fact, he practically growls.

"Fast," I demand. "Hard and fast and now. Oh, please, now."

He doesn't disappoint, and he is inside me in seconds, deep and hard and wonderful. But it's not enough. I want more. Need more. And so I take my arms from around his neck and grab his jacket to pull it off, wanting to get down to skin. Wanting to feel him hard and smooth against me.

And then my fingers touch the rip. The slice in his leather jacket from the fuerie's whip.

I freeze. I just—freeze.

"Christina?"

I shake my head, realizing that this isn't about being a warrior or being horny or wild or any of that.

This is fear.

Fear that I will lose this man.

Fear that this life that I have—that I have back—will be ripped away from me again.

Fear that I will lose everything I've finally grabbed onto.

And, yes, fear that I cannot stop this weapon that is now rising inside me. That I have foolishly triggered.

"Mal. *Mal.*"

I rip his jacket off. I yank his shirt open

and tug it free of his jeans. I need him. Him. *Him.*

He is still inside me, and I don't know if it is the rising terror or the passion that is edging far too close to climax. But I do know that the weapon is rising, wild and hot and fast, and I can barely hold a coherent thought, but I know enough to know that I've gone too far. That this time the attack worked. It wasn't just Mal's jacket the fuerie ripped—it was me. It was the weapon.

It was the fabric of the fucking universe.

Nothing makes sense because I'm losing my grip, and I'm scared. So scared.

Oh please, no, no, no …

My body starts to shake, to heat. It's as if I'm turning inside out, going supernova, turning into something wild.

I clutch at Mal, holding onto his back, my hands buried beneath his shirt as I breathe and fight, breathe and live.

And though I do not understand how or why, I see the world overlaid upon Mal's room, as if I'm looking at a projection of a map on a wall. I see places. I see sparks. I see energy.

It doesn't make any sense, and yet somehow I know. I just *know*.

I understand it now, this weapon that has been a part of me for so long. That has finally risen up far enough to make my acquaintance.

And even as I think those thoughts I can't help but wonder why the hell I'm not dead. Why the world isn't destroyed.

Then I see Mal.

His face is strained, drawn tight with pain.

And when he opens his eyes, they are not gray but red, burning and wild and as bright as the sun.

He's pulling back the weapon.

He'd said he couldn't, but like me, Mal is stronger than he thinks, and he has pulled it down. Taking not just my energy, but energy from the weapon itself.

And even as I realize that, everything shifts again.

My skin no longer feels hot.

The map that had glazed the world disappears.

And Mal's eyes fade back to gray.

With a sigh, we both fall to the ground, as if nothing so weak as human flesh could hold us upright.

"You did it." I barely have a voice, I'm so exhausted. "You pulled the weapon down."

"Just barely," he says. "I didn't think I could—it was almost too much."

"But it wasn't." I manage to roll to him. To press my head against his chest. "You saved me. You saved the world."

He doesn't smile, but I see the way his eyes crinkle with pleasure. "Maybe," he says. "Maybe I did."

"I know where they are." The words spill out of me.

"What? Who?"

I sit up, my head spinning a little bit. "The fuerie. I saw them. I *can* see them."

I don't understand how, but I can feel

the change in me. As if the weapon added something to my make-up. And even though the map has faded and the weapon is no longer rising, I know that I find the map again. That I can see what needs to be seen.

He is sitting up now, too. "Tell me exactly what you're talking about."

I explain what happened. "And I saw them. Spread out over what seemed like a map of the world. And it was covered with pulses. That's their energy, I'm sure of it." I draw in a breath, studying his face. "It's not that hard to believe. It's like what Dante does. I can feel them. Only not just nearby. Everywhere."

"Can you feel them now?"

I take a deep breath and look inside myself, suddenly afraid that I was wrong and this isn't a lingering gift. A little surprise perk from the devil inside me.

But it is there. It's really still there.

I open my eyes and meet his. "Yes." The word is almost a whisper. "It's more of a blur than it was earlier. But I'll learn to focus in."

"Will you?"

I nod. "I don't know how, but I'm certain. This weapon's been in me a long time. Maybe all this time I've been slowly learning how it works."

His brow furrows as he considers my words. "Do you realize what this means?"

I do. "It means we can find them. We can destroy them." I lick my lips. "But Mal, there are a lot of them."

He takes my hands. "There have always been a lot of them. Because of you, we know where they are."

"There's more. To tell you, I mean."

His eyes narrow. "What?"

"I see something else, too. Something different. Something close."

"How close?"

I scoot over so that my back is against the wall and pull my knees up to my chest. I wait until he sits up too and is looking at me. "On Manhattan."

He cocks his head to the side. "What is

it?"

"The amulet. At least, I think it is." I run my fingers through my hair. "What I don't understand is how I can sense it. I mean, it's just a rock, right?"

"Gemstones contain energy. There's a reason folks say there's fire in a diamond, after all. And stones can even trap sentient energy—that's why we need all seven to bind the fuerie. And don't forget about Solomon. He trapped a demon in a ring that had one hell of a gemstone."

He starts to push himself up off the floor.

"Where are you going?"

"I need to talk to Liam. Tomorrow, you're briefing everyone."

"But—"

"What?"

I shake my head. "Nothing." I've got more to tell him, because I've figured out how the weapon works. What it is, deep down at its core. But that doesn't matter right now. Right now, there's a new path. A new plan. And I understand that he can't wait to share that news with his co-leader.

"Go," I say. "But hurry back to me."

He bends over to brush a kiss over my lips. Then he turns around and bends down for his jacket that I'd dropped on the ground. "I'll pass if off to Jessica. Surely she knows someone who can fix the damn thing."

I don't answer. How can I when my entire world has been rocked by what I've just seen?

Mal's back.

Right where I touched him. Right where I clung to him.

Right there on his left side where there used to be a fabulous tattoo of a phoenix.

Now there is just clear, perfect skin.

Some of his lost lives—the ones that went into the burn—he has them back.

I shiver. Because what I know—what I haven't yet told Mal—is that the thing inside me isn't just a weapon.

It's life.

But I know better than anyone that life can be dangerous, too.

CHAPTER 11

"**T**HAT'S PRETTY DAMNED amazing," Dante says after Mal and I have relayed the story to the group.

"Understatement," Jessica says, and the rest of us have to agree with her.

We're in the VIP room at Dark Pleasures, and Mal stands now to pace. "Liam and I talked through the options last night, and then again with Christina this morning. The purpose of this meeting is both information and to put a new mission plan on the table."

"Use Christina to eradicate the rest of the fuerie?" Dagny asks. "Sounds good to me."

"Glad you think so," Mal says. "Because that's about the sum of it."

"So where are they?" Callie asks. "Is there going to be a run tonight?"

"Not tonight," I say. "I have to learn how to pinpoint locations, but I can see enough right now to know there are no fuerie currently on the island of Manhattan."

Everyone looks at Dante, who closes his eyes for a moment, then nods. "I don't have the same range, obviously, but I don't see any nearby either."

"Christina is going to start daily practice," Liam says. "She's going to work on focus and control. And based on what she sees, we're going to be planning and implementing bi-weekly missions."

I nod agreement. "I'm hoping to get the hang of it sooner rather than later. And then maybe the missions can be more frequent, with calls going out to the other offices too, of course."

Raine leans back in his chair. "This really is pretty fucking incredible."

"Yeah," I say. "It is." Despite the fact that the reason I can do this is because there is a nasty weapon hidden inside me, I can't deny that it is nice to have a purpose again. To truly be part of the team.

"Christina won't be going into the field," Liam says. "And of course she's still under strict protection until we can extract the weapon."

Raine shifts in his chair. "Speaking of, what about the amulet?"

"That's something else that Christina can see," Mal says.

"Not all the time, though," I point out. "I saw it clearly last night, but this morning I haven't seen it at all."

"Why not?" The question is from Asher, and it's the only question he's asked during the entire meeting.

"I don't know," I admit. "This is all new to me, too. But I'm guessing it's experience again. Once I learn how to use my handy new map skills, I'll be better able to locate things. Or people."

"Or maybe it wasn't the amulet you saw last night," he suggests.

"It's out there," I say firmly. "And it's close. I can feel it. And I will find it."

Asher is still looking at me, his mouth a thin line, his eyes hard and flat. I expect him to ask another question, but he says nothing. Finally, he leans back in his chair and steeples his fingers on the table.

I feel like I should shout out that the prosecution rests.

I shove away the thought—and turn to Mal so that Asher is no longer in my line of sight.

Mal smiles at me and nods, the motion barely there. But it's enough to let me know that he thinks I did good. And to me, that's the best thing I've heard all day.

After the meeting adjourns, I go to him, taking comfort in the tight press of his arms around me.

"I need to talk with Liam for a while. You want to wait here for me?"

"No, thanks. I'm going to go back to

your place."

"Our place," he says, and I make a face.

"In that case, we need to go get my clothes. I can't keep raiding Callie's closet. Poor Brayden's going to forget he even has a best friend."

"We'll go later today, okay?"

I nod, because that sounds great. "It needs to be after dinner. I got a text earlier. Jefferson is sending his assistant over with some sketches and fabric swatches for the costumes, and I don't want to miss him."

"We'll make a night of it," he says. "Maybe Bray and Dagny will want to grab a bite."

I grin, thinking that sounds like a wonderful idea.

"Soon," he says, then bends to kiss me.

I hold him off. "I need to tell you something else. And you need to tell Liam."

Immediately, his expression shifts to business mode. "All right. Go."

"I know how the weapon works. It's life."

His brow furrows. "What do you mean?"

"It doesn't explode so much as remake everything," I say. "It destroys everything down to the molecular level, then starts it all up again." I don't feel like I'm doing a good job explaining so I try a different tact. "Think of it like that device in the *Star Trek* movie. Did you see it? The one with Khan?"

He's looking at me like I'm insane.

I cock my head. "No way. You've been alive how long and you haven't seen *The Wrath of Khan*?"

"Christina."

I hear the warning in his voice and press on. "Anyway, that's what it does. It's a weapon in that it destroys. But at the same time it rebuilds." I make a face. "From a pragmatic standpoint it doesn't matter to us because we're still dead. Although maybe the brotherhood wouldn't be—I have no idea how the weapon would interact with phoenix fire."

"Not well, I'd imagine," he says. "So you

think this is why you can see the fuerie? Because the weapon is tied to a life-force?"

"No. I think that's why I could give you back some of your life."

He doesn't react. He doesn't even blink. He just stands there a moment, and then says, "What the hell are you talking about?"

"I pressed my hand to your back," I explain. "When the weapon was rising. When it was in all of me. My skin. My cells. When I was glowing."

"You touched my back?"

"Yes." I draw in a breath. "Mal, one of your tats is gone. It's just gone. You're not as close to the hollow as you were. The weapon pulled you back. It's life, don't you see? Brutal and dangerous, yes. But there's some serious potential there."

He's staring at me with the oddest expression. "Yeah," he finally says. "There's one hell of a lot of potential."

BACK IN MAL'S brownstone, I consider how to spend my alone time.

A bath springs to mind, because Mal has a tub big enough to swim in. But somehow going it alone doesn't have the same appeal.

A nap is also an option, because the truth is that I'm tired, but I really don't want to curl up in that wonderful, soft bed without a wonderful, hard man beside me.

I consider exploring the house—he's only given me a quick tour so far, and there's a lot to see on six stories, but that's something else I'd rather do with Mal by my side. Plus, I don't want to seem like a snoop.

Finally, I decide to make popcorn, sit at the kitchen table, and work on memorizing my lines.

Tasty and productive, and after thirty minutes, I'm so into rehearsing that I've not only forgotten about the popcorn, but I barely hear the doorbell.

The second time it rings, I jump in the chair.

Jefferson's sketches.

"Coming!" My shout echoes through the second floor, but I seriously doubt it makes it down to the front door. And since I really don't want Jefferson's assistant to leave, I race downstairs in bare feet, then skid to a stop at the door. It's the old fashioned kind with a little door-covered window instead of a peephole, and I open it and peer out. A short bald man is there with a package. He holds it up, and I can see the Story Street logo.

"Ms. Hart? I've got a package for you from Jefferson Slade."

"Fab," I say, then open the door. I take one step out, then reach for the pen he hands me to sign for the package. Only it's not a pen. It's a needle, and the bald man is jabbing it into my arm.

Almost instantaneously, the world turns black and my knees give out.

I feel myself falling into the bald man's arms, and though I open my mouth to call out for Mal, I'm pretty sure that no sound comes out.

MAL TOSSED BACK the last of his scotch, then slid off the bar stool. He and Liam had just finished talking, and there was no denying that Christina's information about the nature of the weapon was a big fucking deal.

All of it was—the fact that the weapon was life-based rather than destruction-based. And Christina's apparent ability to erase the effects of the phoenix fire.

The first he'd revealed to Liam.

The second, Mal was keeping to himself. At least for a little while.

It was only the second time he'd kept a secret from Liam, and the first had been about Christina, too. Just a few days ago, actually, when Mal had first seen her and chosen not to kill her.

He'd eventually revealed that one to his brothers.

This new secret though—well, this one he intended to hold onto a little bit longer.

He needed to be certain that her ability wasn't just a one time thing. And he needed to be absolutely positive that she could access the ability without endangering herself or the world.

Right now, though, he wanted an hour of not thinking about it. Of not thinking about anything, actually.

All he wanted to do was get home and hold her, and he headed toward the door with that goal firmly in his mind.

He didn't make it.

Instead, he was waylaid by Raine.

"Sorry I was an ass the other day," Raine said, and Mal knew he was referring to Mal's decision to have Dante tail Christina home one night before she and Mal were together. Unobtrusive but necessary protection. "I understand why you sent him instead of me. I just don't like it."

Mal pulled out a chair and sat across the chessboard from his friend. "None of us like it," he said. "We'd like it less if you end up hollow."

"Yeah. True that." He lifted his glass in silent toast to Mal and then downed his scotch. "I have to say you two look good together."

"So do you and Callie," Mal said.

Raine's eyes lit up. "I don't know how I survived before her." He made a face. "Oh, wait. I didn't survive. I was like the walking dead until I had her in my arms." He ran a finger through his hair. "I was such a damn idiot, taking stupid risks. And now every day I'm afraid I'm going to lose her. And she's afraid of it, too. Do you know she doesn't even want me taking my bike out?" he asked, referring to his very sweet motorcycle.

"She just worries," Mal said.

"Oh, I get it. She's worth any sacrifice I have to make. But that doesn't mean I don't miss getting into it. Getting my hands dirty."

Mal said nothing.

"It's just that if I was a mortal cop or fireman, would anyone be making a big deal about me going on patrol or heading off to fight a fire?"

"Probably not," Mal said. "But in our situation, you wouldn't just be dead, man. You'd be gone. Mentally checked out forever. How would she deal with that? Even if you told her now to move on, do you think she could or would? You know she wouldn't. You're her world now. The pain you felt when you thought she was gone, that's what she'll feel if you're lost in the hollow."

"I know. I get it." Raine picked up the black king and rolled it between his fingers. "I didn't think anything scared me anymore. But that does. The possibility that I could end up in the hollow and leave her alone. That's what I hate. That's what I fear." He met Mal's eyes. "Christ I love her."

Mal nodded, thinking of Christina. "Believe me. I know how you feel."

Raine dropped the king back on the table. "Well, fuck."

"Listen," Mal said. Maybe it would be more prudent to wait, but he was going with his gut here, and his gut said that Raine needed some hope. "There's something I need to tell you."

He never got the words out. Before he had a chance to say another word, Callie burst through the door.

"She's gone! The front door is open, and Christina's gone!"

CHAPTER 12

P^{*AIN.*}
    Burning, horrible, screaming, fire-breathing pain.

I have no idea where I am when I come to. I barely know my own name.

There is just the pain and the fear.

And the weapon rising inside me.

Oh fuck. Oh shit.

Instinctively, I try to run, but I'm strapped to some sort of pole. I struggle, but that only seems to make the bonds tighter.

I blink, trying to see, but the room is dark.

Then I realize it's not dark, it's just that my vision is gray, as if dulled by the pain that still fills me. Still grows. Still pushes the weapon up.

I'm in what looks to be a warehouse, only it is empty. There is only me, the little bald man who assaulted me, and two other men in dark jackets and unshaven faces.

I remember what Mal said during the briefing about how the fuerie recruit humans. Maybe there were no fuerie on Manhattan, but there sure as hell were some minions.

I try to focus on the bald man. "You don't really work for Jefferson, do you?" My voice is like gravel and so low that I doubt that he can even hear me.

"Stupid bitch."

I take it back. He can hear me.

I am floating. The world turning inside out. Pain so potent I'm no longer sure it's real.

"Knock her out again. They said she couldn't wake up. Bad shit if she wakes up."

It's one of the unshaven men. He's standing across the room. A room that looks like a checkerboard. It's covered with a grid of wire and cable, and I seem to be right in the middle.

The focal point.

The center of attention.

Ground fucking zero.

"Now, dammit. Look at her. She's starting to turn colors."

Pain and power.

It's rising.

Rising.

And the bald man is coming at me and he has a needle and he's going to stick me with it and I cannot get away because I'm tied to a post.

And then he's right there.

And the needle is against my flesh.

And I cry out for Mal. I scream his name.

Malcolm, Malcolm, Malcolm.

It echoes through this empty warehouse and is the last thing I hear before the world turns black.

THE MOMENT CALLIE burst into the lounge, Mal had turned numb, the world reduced to only two elements—action and revenge.

Raine had stood, but Mal had dismissed him with a look. "No," he'd said. "I'm not risking both of you."

Mal hadn't stayed to argue. He knew that Liam would back him. He'd just pressed forward, mind and body on autopilot. Moving fast. Moving efficiently.

And thanking the goddamn universe that every time Christina was born into this world, he could sense her essence.

Only the most fundamental of thoughts went through his head:

She was close.

Gather the team.

Pull the weapons.

Find her.

Save her.

"No fuerie nearby," Dante had confirmed. "Must have used humans to grab her."

Mal hadn't said anything. He'd continued to move, confident the team would follow, all except Raine and Callie. Raine, who was staying to keep him safe from the burn. Callie, who was staying because of inexperience.

They found the warehouse in less than twenty minutes. Fast. Efficient. Just like any other mission. At least until Liam put his hand on Mal's shoulder. "We'll get her."

Mal only nodded. That much was a given, because not getting her simply wasn't an option.

Liam had already turned his attention to the rest of the team. "We go in hot," he said. "Cover Mal. Take out as many as you can. Stay alive as long as you can. But this mission can't be pretty and we can't take our time. Not when the clock is literally ticking." He looked at each of them in turn. "Go."

They went—and it was a goddamn clusterfuck. Bullets flying. Bodies falling. Jessica first, then Dante. And both Liam and Ash took hits, as did Mal, though the sting of the bullet in his shoulder was nothing when weighed against his fear.

In the end, they took out all the furies' minions who had been guarding the warehouse. Then, with Liam and Ash in his wake, Mal burst inside, expecting to see another army of minions in the interior.

But there were no minions in the dilapidated warehouse. No warriors. No bad guys.

No one except Christina.

She was trapped in the center of a wire grid that was buzzing and humming with power. She was held fast like a fly in a web. Her body shook violently, pain filling her, and the weapon going hot.

A terror that he hadn't experienced in centuries tore through Mal as he watched Christina's skin burn a translucent yellow-red, like the image that remains after looking too long at the sun.

She was on fire—literally—a live weapon. A goddamn dangerous one.

And there was no fucking way he could

get to her.

He was going to lose her.

"Christina!"

No response. No recognition.

All he saw on her face was pain.

Dear Christ, he was really going to lose her. And the whole goddamn universe on top of that.

Because this was it. This was the fuerie's final play. Torture Christina. Release the weapon. Reform the fabric of the universe.

Game. Fucking. Over.

No.

Somehow, he was going to save her. *They* were going to save her.

The problem was *how.*

And the answer was power.

"We need to get this goddamn thing shut down, and fast," he yelled to Ash.

"On it," Ash called back, and he realized that both Liam and Ash had climbed up to the catwalk and were searching for a way to do that very thing.

"Where's Dagny?" Mal called.

"Status unknown," Liam said.

Mal cursed, hoping that she was outside. Hoping that she was thinking along the same lines and was looking for a way to cut the power.

Because the only way to get to Christina was to traverse the grid.

But that, of course, would kill him.

Under other circumstances that wouldn't be a problem, as he'd just regenerate. But in this case, there was no time. Soon enough she'd reach the tipping point, and this would be all over.

"Mal…"

Relief swept over him as her thin voice reached out to him from across the cavernous space.

"I'm coming, lover. Just hold on. Baby, just hold on."

"Can't hold—hurts—so tired…"

He clenched his fists, willing himself to *think, dammit, think*. There had to be a way. There had to be something he was missing.

Even as the thought entered his mind,

the building went dark.

Dagny! She'd shut off the power!

For an instant, relief flooded Mal, only to fade the moment he realized that the wire web was still hot.

"It's on a different system." Ash called down to Mal from the catwalk. "There's got to be a separate power source for the grid, but I'm not seeing it."

"Look harder," Mal growled, even as he skirted along the edge of the web, looking for a power source extending across the floor.

"There!" Liam's voice filled the space. He was on the catwalk, too, on the opposite side from Ash, and now he pointed down toward the web. Toward Christina.

"Oh, fuck," Mal said. He hadn't seen it before, but he should have. The power that fed the web came from thick cables that extended up through the concrete floor.

Goddammit, he should have brought Raine. Maybe he could have talked to the goddamn power source and convinced it to shut itself down.

But Raine was back at Number 36, and the only way to get to the cables was to traverse the grid—but if he did that, he'd die.

And fuck it all, he was going to do that anyway, because just a few feet away, Christina was vibrating with the force of the power building within her, and even the tips of her hair were beginning to glow red.

"Out of time! Out of time!" Mal shouted. "Ideas!"

"I'm shorting this fucker out," Liam called back. "It's got to have a secondary power source—they wouldn't leave it unprotected—so it'll kick back on even if I manage to short it out. But I should be able to buy you some time."

"And I'll buy you a little more," Ash said. "I'll jump as soon as it flickers back on. That gives you one outage to get across the web, and another to get her out of there and under control."

"*Malcolm!*" Christina's scream echoed

around them.

"Now!" Mal shouted to Liam, who threw himself from the catwalk onto the grid, snapping some of the wires as he did so, then screaming in pain as his body writhed with the wild and violent voltage. Immediately the grid sparked and snapped—

—and fuck if Liam wasn't right. The whole thing shut down for one goddamn precious moment.

Christina, however, didn't shut down. She still sizzled and popped.

"It's too late," Ash called, as Mal raced toward her, leaping from square to square in the perverted chessboard of a floor that separated him from the woman he loved. "The weapon's armed. Mal, shit, you'll never pull it back."

Mal knew damn well that Ash was probably right—but he really didn't give a fuck. "Either way we're dead," he shouted back. "I've got to at least try."

Ash didn't answer. The grid had started

to spark back on, and instead of speaking, he flung himself down, landing near Liam's body in the middle of the grid, his neck snapping even as the grid fizzled and went dormant again.

Thank god.

And then—oh thank god—he was at her. But she was wild, on fire, and when he pulled her close, the heat of her burned his skin raw.

"*Christina.*" He held her against him, ignoring the pain as his clothes began to burn. He needed to hear her voice. But she was too far gone, and when the power grid surged back on beneath him, Mal cried out in fresh pain and horror, because he couldn't survive this. He couldn't—

And then it stopped, and he sucked in a breath as he realized that the web had shorted out once again, this time because of the phoenix fire rising around both Ash and Liam.

Mal saw it, acknowledged it, but didn't think about it. All he could think about was

Christina. All he could do was hold her, claim her, draw her in. Find her energy and pull it down, down, down.

Except it didn't matter. Not this time. This wasn't her energy, it was the weapon.

And it wasn't just a tiny peek as it had been that night she'd erased part of the tat from his back. This was huge. This was the world. This was the fucking Big Bang, and he was absorbing it. Pulling it in. Letting *his* body take it. Letting *his* being support that power. Taking it. Taking everything he had to and more—because he could endure anything to get Christina back. Hadn't he been enduring hell all these years for her?

How much worse could saving her be?

And then he felt the power inside him. Filling him. Drowning him. Controlling him. And *oh god oh Christ* how the hell was he supposed to tamp it down? Because now he was the weapon and it was going to all end soon.

He was the weapon, and there would be no coming back from this death.

No friends.

No life.

No love.

No Christina.

This was the end. And the end was horrible.

HE IS HERE he is here he is here.

The words fill my mind, fighting through the pain. Twining with this rising power. This explosive force.

It's wild and intense and uncontrollable—and it is right here, about to burst free. Opening, opening...

And yet...

And yet I can't let it win. I can't let go.

I can't give in to the pain and the fear and the horror. Not without trying. Not without clinging to him.

Not without trying to help him pull it down, down, down, just the way he taught me. Holding it in. Keeping it down. Giving him my strength the way he would give me his until the pounding slows and the heat begins to die and the rush that fills my head calms and I can breathe and—

Almost.

Almost.

The world that had been red and black starts to regain color. The wildness within me starts to recede.

Then we are floating. Moving. I realize as if in a dream that we are being carried, and I look up and see that Ash and Liam are holding us, moving us.

They put us gently on the floor away from the wire grid, and Jessica is kneeling over Mal, her hands on him, and his skin is glowing, the burns fading.

And his skin is clear. Just one tiny tat remains, a small phoenix that marks him as a member of the brotherhood.

That is when I realize. That is when I know.

We did it. We really did it.

We pulled it back.

Mal took the weapon. He drew in the energy. He absorbed the life force.

And he shut it down. With my strength to bolster him, he shut it down.

We survived.

And yet as my heavy eyelids droop, pulling me down into the sweet relief of sleep, I cannot hold back the one final thought that rattles in my mind: *We survived, yes. But barely.*

CHAPTER 13

I AWAKEN TO find myself in a thin nightgown on an unfamiliar bed. I am still wrapped in Mal's arms. He is smiling down at me, his eyes heavy as if he has just awakened, too.

"Where are we?"

He looks around. "Guest apartment in Number 36. Jessica and Liam use it sometimes. She's probably keeping an eye on us. Making sure everything heals the way it's supposed to."

I nod, then sit up. I stay like that for a moment, and then I stand. I remember my last thoughts before I passed out at the warehouse, and I know what I need to say.

I'm just not entirely sure how to say it.

There is a light tap on the door, and Mal calls out, "Come in."

I expect Jessica, but it is Ash. "Thought I heard you two moving around. Need anything?"

I shake my head. Right now, I just need him to leave.

He glances at Mal, who is looking only at me.

"Where's Jessica?" I ask.

"Busy with Dagny. Power grid was boo-by-trapped. Jessica's got her set up in the den. She'll be fine, but there are a lot of wounds to tend. I said I'd hang out for a while. Give Jessica a hand with whatever she needs."

I nod, but say no more, and after a moment, he leaves.

I stay as I am for a moment, watching the closed door, remembering back to the way Ash had tried to kill me not so very long ago.

Full circle, I think, and then turn to face Mal.

"I love you," I say.

I watch the pleasure on his face, and the way he adjusts to sit up in the bed, as if the words alone have given him strength.

"I love you," I repeat, because the words are true and they no longer frighten me. "I'm sorry I haven't said that before."

"I'm glad to hear it now. But at the same time, I'm a little wary."

I look at the floor. I should have known he would say something like that. Because doesn't Mal always see through me?

"I can't stay," I say, because there is no point in dragging this out. "You taught me some control, and I'm sure I could learn more. And god knows I enjoy the lessons. But it will never be enough. They used pain—real, horrible, violent pain—to shatter my control. To draw the weapon out. And they did, Mal. They did pull it out of me. If you hadn't been there—if you'd been a few minutes later or if Liam and Ash hadn't shut down the grid—"

I cut myself off, because the end of the world is too horrible to speak.

"We're cursed, you and I," I continue. "Star-crossed. But we've been so blessed to have the time that we have had together."

"No." It is just one word, but it is powerful.

I shake my head, fighting to keep steady. Fighting not to give in.

"Yes," I say. "You have to let me go. It's not forever, Mal. We know how this works. We'll find each other again."

"No," he repeats. "Hell no." He tosses the blanket aside and slides out of the bed. He is wearing a pair of black silk pajama bottoms that are so big around the waist that I assume they are Liam's. "I swore to protect you." He strides toward me. "To cherish you. And yet I repeatedly destroyed you."

"You did what you had to do."

"Bullshit. I took the easy path. Over and over and over."

"Easy? If it was easy, then kill me now, Mal. Take your fire sword and thrust it through my heart." I close the distance between us and stroke his cheek. Just touching him comforts me, but I force myself to remain focused. I have to do this. There is no other option. "Do you think I don't know how hard it was for you? The sacrifice you made? Do you think I don't realize how much easier I had it, me without my memories? With non-existence and then with no memory. A fresh life every time?"

I shake my head. "No, I understand pain, Mal." I draw in a breath. "And that's why I won't ask you to do it again."

"Thank god."

"But I do have to die."

I see the confusion in his eyes.

"I'm asking Ash," I say, and then call out for the other man.

He must have been right outside the door, because he enters almost immediately.

"No," Mal says to me, even as I say to Ash, "You were right."

I glance at Mal. "He knows it, too. But he can't do it."

"*Won't* do it," Mal says. "And neither will you," he says to Ash. "Or I will end you so many times you'll wake up greeting the hollow."

I draw in a breath, but otherwise ignore that. To his credit, Ash looks unfazed. And why not? I already know that he's on my side here.

"Please," I say to Ash. "I need you to do this. And he knows that it needs to be done."

Ash takes a single step toward me. Behind me, Mal's hand grips my shoulder.

"No."

I blink, confused. I am certain that Ash couldn't have said that word. It must have come from Mal, and I'm just confused from my near-end-of-the-universe experience.

"What?"

"No," he repeats, even as Mal's hand on my shoulder loosens. "You said that what's in you isn't just a weapon, but a map?"

"I—" I look between him and Mal. "Well, yes."

"And you can find the fuerie. All over the globe? Just like you said at the meeting."

"Well, yeah. I mean, I have to concentrate. Call it up. But—yes."

"And the amulet? You can find the seventh amulet?"

"I can."

"Then I don't see any reason to abandon the plan," Ash says. "We use you to find the amulet. We get the weapon the fuck out of you." He looks to Mal. "Work for you?"

I turn so that I can see Mal's face—and the smile when he nods at his friend. His brother. "Yeah," Mal says. "I think that will work just fine."

"All right, then," Asher says, and then leaves, shutting the door firmly behind him.

"Mal…" I trail off, not sure what to say.

He pulls me into his arms and wipes away a tear with the pad of his thumb.

"I'm so glad to still be here, but I'm terrified it's a mistake."

"It's not."

"I love you." I draw a tremulous breath, drawing strength from this man who completes me. "All these years and we've had so little time."

"We'll have more," Mal promises me. "We'll have forever."

I nod and kiss him and let him pull me close.

But the fear is still there. Because unless we find the amulet—unless we find it soon—I cannot stay.

And while leaving would break my heart, I know that in the end I will not remember.

It is Mal who will remain behind. Mal who will suffer. Mal who will wait out the years until I am born again and he can find me once more.

I don't want that for him. I don't want to make him suffer anymore than he already has.

But I know the stakes.

And I am terribly afraid that in the end I will have no choice but to hurt the man that I love.

I hope you enjoyed the second part of Mal and Christina's story, which follows Part 1, Find Me in Darkness. I'd be thrilled if you'd leave a review at your favorite retailer!

And be sure to find out what happens next for these star-crossed lovers in Find Me in Passion!

And if you missed Callie and Raine's story, Caress of Darkness, be sure to grab a copy now!

Finally, don't close this book yet! Keep reading for the first chapter of Caress of Darkness...

Please enjoy this first chapter from Raine and Callie's story:

CARESS OF DARKNESS

A Dark Pleasures novella

By

Julie Kenner

CHAPTER 1

"WHO THE FUCK are you?"

I jump, startled by the voice—deep and male and undeniably irritated—that echoes across the forest of boxes scattered throughout my father's SoHo antique store.

"Who am I?" I repeat as I stand and search the shadows for the intruder. "Who the hell are you?"

There is more bravado in my voice than I feel, especially when I finally see the man who has spoken. He is standing in the shadows near the front door—a door that I am damn sure I locked after putting the Closed sign in the window and settling in for a long night of inventory and packing.

He is tall, well over six feet, with a lean, muscular build that is accentuated by the faded jeans that hug his thighs and the simple white T-shirt that reveals muscled arms sleeved with tattoos.

His casual clothes, inked skin, and close-shaved head hint at danger and rebellion, but those traits are contrasted by a commanding, almost elegant, presence that seems to both fill the room and take charge of it. This is a man who would be equally at ease in a tux as a T-shirt. A man who expects the world to bend to his will, and if it doesn't comply, he will go out and bend it himself.

I see that confidence most potently in his face, all sharp lines and angles that blend together into a masterpiece now dusted with the shadow of a late afternoon beard. He has the kind of eyes that miss nothing, and right now they are hard and assessing. They are softened, however, by the kind of long, dark lashes that most women would kill for.

His mouth is little more than a hard slash across his features, but I see a hint of softness, and when I find myself wondering how those lips would feel against my skin, I realize that I have been staring and yank myself firmly from my reverie.

"I asked you a question," I snap, more harshly than I intended. "Who are you, and how did you get in here?"

"Raine," he says, striding toward me. "Rainer Engel. And I walked in through the front door."

"I locked it." I wipe my now-sweaty hands on my dusty yoga pants.

"The fact that I'm inside suggests otherwise."

He has crossed the store in long, efficient strides, and now stands in front of me. I catch his scent, all musk and male, sin and sensuality, and feel an unwelcome ache between my thighs.

Not unwelcome because I don't like sex. On the contrary, I'd have to label myself a fan, and an overenthusiastic one at that.

Because the truth is that I've spent too many nights in the arms of too many strangers trying to fill some void in myself.

I say "some void" because I don't really know what I'm searching for. A connection, I guess, but at the same time I'm scared of finding one and ending up hurt, which is why I shy from traditional "my friend has a friend" kind of dating, and spend more time than I should in bars and clubs. And that means that while I might be enjoying a series of really good lays, I'm not doing anything more than using sex as a Band-Aid.

At least, that is what my therapist, Kelly, back home in Austin says. And since I'm a lawyer and not a shrink, I'm going to have to take her word on that.

"We're closed," I say firmly. Or, rather, I intend to say firmly. In fact, my voice comes out thin, suggesting a question rather than a command.

Not that my tone matters. The man— *Raine*—seems entirely uninterested in what I have to say.

He cocks his head slightly to one side, as if taking my measure, and if the small curve of that sensual mouth is any indication, he likes what he sees. I prop a hand on my hip and stare back defiantly. I know what I look like—and I know that with a few exceptions, men tend to go stupid when I dial it up.

The ratty law school T-shirt I'm wearing is tight, accenting breasts that I'd cursed in high school, but that had become a boon once I started college and realized that my ample tits, slender waist, and long legs added up to a combination that made guys drool. Add in wavy blonde hair and green eyes and I've got the kind of cheerleader-esque good looks that make so many of the good old boy lawyers in Texas think that I've got cotton candy for brains.

And believe me when I say that I'm not shy about turning their misogynistic stereotype to my advantage, both in the courtroom and out of it.

"You're Callie." His voice conveys absolute certainty, as if his inspection confirmed one of the basic facts of the universe. Which, since I *am* Callie, I guess it did. But how the hell he knows who I am is beyond me.

"Your father talks about you a lot," Raine says, apparently picking up on my confusion. His eyes rake over me as he speaks, and my skin prickles with awareness, as potent as if his fingertip had stroked me. "A lawyer who lives in Texas with the kind of looks that make a father nervous, balanced by sharp, intelligent eyes that reassure him that she's not going to do anything stupid."

"You know my father."

"I know your father," he confirms.

"And he told you that about me?"

"The lawyer part. The rest I figured out all on my own." One corner of his mouth curves up. "I have eyes, after all." Those eyes are currently aimed at my chest, and I say a silent thank you to whoever decided that padded bras were a good thing because otherwise he would certainly see how hard and tight my nipples have become.

"University of Texas School of Law. Good school." He lifts his gaze from my chest to my face, and the heat I see in those ice blue eyes seems to seep under my skin, melting me a bit from the inside out. "Very good."

I lick my lips, realizing that my mouth has gone uncomfortably dry. I've been working as an assistant district attorney for the last two years. I've gotten used to being the one in charge of a room. And right now, I'm feeling decidedly off-kilter, part of me wanting to pull him close, and the other wanting to run as far and as fast from him as I can.

Since neither option is reasonable at the moment, I simply take a step back, then find myself trapped by the glass jewelry case, now pressing against my ass.

I clear my throat. "Listen, Mr. Engel, if you're looking for my father—"

"I am, and I apologize for snapping at you when I came in, but I was surprised to see that the shop was closed, and when I saw someone other than Oliver moving inside, I got worried."

"I closed early so that I could work without being interrupted."

A hint of a smile plays at his mouth. "In that case, I'll also apologize for interrupting. But Oliver asked me to come by when I got back in town. I'm anxious to discuss the amulet that he's located."

"Oh." I don't know why I'm surprised. He obviously hadn't come into the store looking for me. And yet for some reason the fact that I've suddenly become irrelevant rubs me the wrong way.

Clearly, I need to get a grip, and I paste on my best customer service smile. "I'm really sorry, but my dad's not here."

"No? I told him I'd come straight over." I can hear the irritation in his voice. "He knows how much I want this piece—how much I'm willing to pay. If he's made arrangements to sell it to another—"

"*No.*" The word is fast and firm and

entirely unexpected. "It's not like that. My dad doesn't play games with clients."

"That's true. He doesn't." His brow creases as he looks around the shop, taking in the open boxes, half filled with inventory, the colored sticky notes I've been using to informally assign items to numbered boxes, and the general disarray of the space. "Callie. What's happened to your father?"

It is the way he says my name that loosens my tongue. Had he simply asked the question, I probably would have told him that he could come back in the morning and we'd search the computerized inventory for the piece he's looking for. But there is something so intimate about my name on his lips that I can't help but answer honestly.

"My dad had a stroke last week." My voice hitches as I speak, and I look off toward the side of the store, too wrecked to meet his eyes directly.

"Oh, Callie." He steps closer and takes my hand, and I'm surprised to find that I not only don't pull away, but that I actually have to fight the urge to pull our joint hands close to my heart.

"I didn't know," he says. "I'm so sorry. How is he doing?"

"N-not very well." I suck in a breath and try to gather myself, but it's just so damn hard. My mom walked out when I was four, saying that being a mother was too much responsibility, and ever since I've been my dad's entire world. It's always amazed me that he didn't despise me. But he really doesn't. He says that I was a gift, and I know it's true because I have seen and felt it every day of my life.

Whatever the cause of my disconnect with men, it doesn't harken back to my dad, a little fact that I know fascinates my shrink, though she's too much the professional to flat out tell me as much.

"Does he have decent care? Do you need any referrals? Any help financially?" Raine is crouching in front of me, and I realize that I have sunk down, so that my butt is on the cold tile floor and I am hugging my knees.

I shake my head, a bit dazed to realize this stranger is apparently offering to help pay my dad's medical bills. "We're fine. He's got great care and great insurance. He's just—" I break off as my voice cracks. "*Shit.*"

"Hey, it's okay. Breathe now. That's it, just breathe." He presses his hands to my shoulders, and his face is just inches away. His eyes are wide and safe and warm, and I want to slide into them. To just disappear into a place where there are neither worries nor responsibilities. Where someone strong will hold me and take care of me and make everything bad disappear.

But that's impossible, and so I draw another breath in time with his words and try once again to formulate a coherent thought. "He's—he's got good doctors, really. But he's not lucid. And this is my dad. I mean, Oliver Sinclair hasn't gone a day in his life without an opinion or a witticism."

I feel the tears well in my eyes and I

swipe them away with a brusque brush of my thumb. "And it kills me because I can look at him and it breaks my heart to know that he must have all this stuff going on inside his head that he just can't say, and—and—"

But I can't get the words out, and I feel the tears snaking down my cheeks, and dammit, dammit, *dammit*, I do not want to lose it in front of this man—this stranger who doesn't feel like a stranger.

His grip on my shoulders tightens and he leans toward me.

And then—oh, dear god—his lips are on mine and they are as warm and soft as I'd imagined and he's kissing me so gently and so sweetly that all my worries are just melting away and I'm limp in his arms.

"Shhh. It's okay." His voice washes over me, as gentle and calming as a summer rain. "Everything's going to be okay."

I breathe deep, soothed by the warm sensuality of this stranger's golden voice. Except he isn't a stranger. I may not have met him before today, but somehow, here in his arms, I *know* him.

And that, more than anything, comforts me.

Calmer, I tilt my head back and meet his eyes. It is a soft moment and a little sweet— but it doesn't stay that way. It changes in the space of a glance. In the instant of a heartbeat. And what started out as gentle comfort transforms into fiery heat.

I don't know which of us moves first. All I know is that I have to claim him and be claimed by him. That I have to taste him— consume him. Because in some essential way that I don't fully understand, I know that only this man can quell the need burning inside me, and I lose myself in the hot intensity of his mouth upon mine. Of his tongue demanding entrance, and his lips, hard and demanding, forcing me to give everything he wants to take.

I am limp against him, felled by the onslaught of erotic sparks that his kisses have scattered through me. I am lost in the sensation of his hands stroking my back. Of his chest pressed against my breasts.

But it isn't until I realize that he has pulled me into his lap and that I can feel the hard demand of his erection against my rear that I force myself to escape this sensual reality and scramble backward out of his embrace.

"I'm sorry," I say, my breath coming too hard.

"Callie—" The need I hear in his voice reflects my own, and I clench my hands into fists as I fight against the instinct to move back into his arms.

"No." I don't understand what's happening—this instant heat, like a match striking gasoline. I've never reacted to a man this way before. My skin feels prickly, as if I've been caught in a lightning storm. His scent is all over me. And the taste of him lingers on my mouth.

And oh, dear god, I'm wet, my body literally aching with need, with a primal desire for him to just rip my clothes off and take me right there on the hard, dusty floor.

He's triggered a wildness in me that I don't understand—and my reaction scares the hell out of me.

"You need to go," I say, and I am astonished that my words are both measured and articulate, as if I'm simply announcing that it is closing time to a customer.

He stays silent, but I shake my head anyway, and hold up a finger as if in emphasis.

"No," I say, in response to nothing. "I don't know anything about this amulet. And now you really need to leave. Please," I add. "Please, Raine. I need you to go."

For a moment he only looks at me. Then he nods, a single tilt of his head in acknowledgment. "All right," he says very softly. "I'll go. But I'm not ever leaving you again."

I stand frozen, as if his inexplicable words have locked me in place. He turns slowly and strides out of the shop without looking back. And when the door clicks into place behind him and I am once again alone, I gulp in air as tears well in my eyes again.

I rub my hands over my face, forgiving myself for this emotional miasma because of all the shit that's happened with my dad. Of course I'm a wreck; what daughter wouldn't be?

Determined to get a grip, I follow his path to the door, then hold onto the knob. I'd come over intending to lock it. But now I have to fight the urge to yank it open and beg him to return.

It's an urge I fight. It's just my grief talking. My fear that I'm about to lose my father, the one person in all the world who is close to me, and so I have clung to a stranger in a desperate effort to hold fast to something.

That, at least, is what my shrink would say. *You're fabricating a connection in order to fill a void. It's what you do, Callie. It's what you've always done when lonely and afraid.*

I nod, telling myself I agree with Kelly's voice in my head.

And I do.

Because I am lonely.

And I am afraid of losing my dad.

But that's not the whole of it. Because there's something else that I'm afraid of, too, though I cannot put my finger on it. A strange sense of something coming. Something dark. Something bad.

And what scares me most is the ridiculous, unreasonable fear that I have just pushed away the one person I need to survive whatever is waiting for me out there in the dark.

Want to read more?

Visit the Dark Pleasures page on Julie's website.
http://juliekenner.com/jks-books/dark-pleasures/

JK'S BOOKLIST

I hope you enjoyed *Find Me in Pleasure*! If you think your friends or other readers would enjoy the book, I'd be honored if you'd rate or "like" the book or leave a review at your favorite retailers. And, of course, I'm always thrilled if you want to spread the word through Twitter, Facebook or other social media outlets.

Questions about the book, or me, or the meaning of the universe? I'd love to hear from you. You can reach me via email at juliekenner@gmail.com or on Twitter (I'm @juliekenner) or through Facebook at www.facebook.com/JulieKennerBooks or www.facebook.com/JKennerBooks

Don't want to miss any of my books or news? Be sure to sign up for my newsletter. You can use this link to the newsletter (http://eepurl.com/-tfoP) or go to my website, www.juliekenner.com

I've written a lot of books, and most of them are available in digital format. Here's a list of just a few (you can find more at my website!); I hope you check them out!

Kate Connor Demon-Hunting Soccer Mom Series that Charlaine Harris, *New York Times* bestselling author of the Sookie Stackhouse / True Blood series, raved "shows you what would happen if Buffy got married and kept her past a secret. It's a hoot."

Carpe Demon

California Demon

Demons Are Forever

The Demon You Know

Deja Demon

Demon Ex Machina

Pax Demonica

The Trouble with Demons

Learn more at

DemonHuntingSoccerMom.com

The Protector (Superhero) Series that *RT Book Review* magazine raves are true originals, "filled with humor, adventure and fun!"

The Cat's Fancy (prequel)

Aphrodite's Kiss

Aphrodite's Passion

Aphrodite's Secret

Aphrodite's Flame

Aphrodite's Embrace

Aphrodite's Delight

Aphrodite's Charms (boxed set)

Dead Friends and Other Dating Dilemmas

Learn more at WeProtectMortals.com

Blood Lily Chronicles

Tainted

Torn

Turned

The Blood Lily Chronicles (boxed set)

Devil May Care Series

Raising Hell

Sure As Hell

Dark Pleasures

Caress of Darkness

Find Me in Darkness

Find Me in Pleasure

Find Me in Passion

Caress of Pleasure

By J. Kenner as J.K. Beck:

Shadow Keepers Series (dark paranormal romance)

When Blood Calls

When Pleasure Rules

When Wicked Craves

When Passion Lies

When Darkness Hungers

When Temptation Burns

Shadow Keepers: Midnight

As J. Kenner:

New York Times **&** *USA Today* **bestselling Stark Trilogy (erotic romance)**

Release Me (a *New York Times* and *USA Today* bestseller)

Claim Me (a #2 *New York Times* bestseller!)

Complete Me (a #2 *New York Times* bestseller!)

Take Me (epilogue novella)

Tame Me (A Stark International novella)

Have Me

Say My Name

On My Knees

New York Times **&** *USA Today* **bestselling *The Most Wanted* series (erotic romance)**

Wanted

Heated

Ignited

Thanks again, and happy reading!

ABOUT JULIE

Author Photo by Kathy Whittaker

A *New York Times*, *USA Today*, *Publishers Weekly*, and *Wall Street Journal* bestselling author, Julie Kenner (aka J. Kenner) writes a range of stories including romance (erotic, sexy, funny & sweet), young adult novels, chick lit suspense and paranormal mommy lit. Her foray into the latter, *Carpe Demon: Adventures of a Demon-Hunting Soccer Mom*, was selected as a Booksense Summer Paperback Pick for 2005, was a Target Breakout Book, was a Barnes & Noble Number One SFF/Fantasy bestseller for seven weeks, and is in development as a feature film with 1492 Pictures.

As J. Kenner, she also writes erotic romance (including the bestselling Stark Trilogy) as well as dark and sexy paranormal romances, including the Shadow Keeper series previously published as J.K. Beck.

You can connect with Julie through her website, www.juliekenner.com, Twitter (@juliekenner) and her Facebook pages at www.facebook.com/juliekennerbooks and www.facebook.com/jkennerbooks.

For all the news on upcoming releases, contests, and other fun stuff, be sure to sign up for her newsletter (http://eepurl.com/-tfoP).

CPSIA information can be obtained at www.ICGtesting.com
Printed in the USA
LVOW07s1804091015

457665LV00013B/180/P